Oddest of All

Oddest of All

STORIES BY
BRUCE COVILLE

HARCOURT, INC.

ORLANDO AUSTIN NEW YORK SAN DIEGO LONDON

"In Our Own Hands" copyright © 1999 by Bruce Coville, originally published in *Bruce Coville's Alien Visitors*, published by Avon/HarperCollins.

"What's the Worst That Could Happen?" copyright © 2003 by Bruce Coville, originally published in *13*, edited by James Howe, published by Atheneum.

"The Ghost Let Go" copyright © 1994 by Bruce Coville, originally published in *Bruce Coville's Book of Ghosts*, published by Apple/Scholastic.

"In the Frog King's Court" copyright © 2000 by Bruce Coville, originally published in *Ribbiting Tales,* edited by Nancy Springer, published by Philomel Books.

"The Thing in Auntie Alma's Pond" copyright © 1996 by Bruce Coville, originally published in *Bruce Coville's Book of Spine Tinglers*, published by Apple/Scholastic.

"The Hardest, Kindest Gift" copyright © 2001 by Bruce Coville, originally published in *Half-Human,* published by Scholastic.

Library of Congress Cataloging-in-Publication Data
Coville, Bruce.
Oddest of all/stories by Bruce Coville.
v. cm.
Summary: A collection of nine short stories featuring ghosts, half-humans, unicorns, and other unusual creatures.
Contents: In our own hands—What's the worst that could happen?— The ghost let go—In the frog king's court—The thing in Auntie Alma's pond— The hardest, kindest gift—The mask of Eamonn Tiyado—Herbert Hutchison in the underworld—The boy with silver eyes—A note from the author.
1. Horror tales, American. 2. Children's stories, American.
[1. Horror stories. 2. Short stories.] I. Title.
PZ7.C8344Ocp 2008
[Fic]—dc22 2007050298
ISBN 978-0-15-205808-1

Text set in Bembo
Designed by Cathy Riggs

First edition
A C E G H F D B

Printed in the United States of America

For Joan and Edward Ormondroyd

Contents

Oddest of All

In Our Own Hands

JULY 22

I am so totally freaked out.

Of course, that is probably true for everyone on the planet.

How could we not be, after what happened this morning?

I was sitting at the kitchen table, sparring with my mother over how much sugar I could put on my breakfast cereal—which is kind of silly for a guy home from college—when it started. The telescreen on the wall made an odd sound. I looked up—and forgot all about the sugar.

The meat puppet who usually reads the morning news had been replaced by a woman who had scaly blue skin and close-cropped green hair. Her ears were much too small for her head, her eyes much too big. Despite all that, she was beautiful, in a weird kind of way.

My first reaction was to laugh, because it was kind of cool. I figured some idiot at the station was playing a joke.

"Someone's going to be in big trouble for this," predicted Mom. "I bet whoever did it gets fired."

We stared at the screen, waiting for the news to come back on. When nothing happened I picked up the remote. But before I could change the channel the woman said, "Greetings, people of Earth."

I burst out laughing. Mom shook her head in disgust. "What a stupid joke. Change the channel, Johnny."

I did.

The woman was still there.

I changed it again, and again, and again.

No matter what channel I turned to—and we get 208 of them—the blue woman was still there. Mom's eyes got wider, and she slid her chair closer to mine. "Johnny! What's going on?"

I shook my head. I had no idea. But a strange feeling—some combination of fear and excitement—was starting to blossom in my stomach.

Finally the blue woman spoke again. "I assume most

of you have now realized that this broadcast is on all channels. That is because the message I bring is for all people, and it is important that as many of you as possible hear it. However, what I have come to tell you will not make sense unless you know two things."

As far as I was concerned, nothing made sense right now.

"First, we are not here to threaten you."

It was such an odd thing to say that I almost laughed again. But part of me was too scared for that. I wished that Dad was here. But he was gone, a victim of the air-quality crisis that had killed so many people the year I was thirteen.

The blue woman spoke again. "Second, you must know that we *can* do what we say. I will now prove that to you. Please do not be frightened. This demonstration is just to help you accept the truth of what I have to tell you."

Mom reached for her coffee. I noticed that her hand was shaking, which made me feel better about my own trembling fingers. Before she could pick up her cup, the light went out. Not the lights. The *light*. Darkness was everywhere, as if the sun itself had disappeared.

"Johnny!" cried my mother.

"Do not be afraid," said the voice from the TV—which was also dark, of course. "We will return the light soon."

I wondered how the TV could work with the power out, until I understood that this was not a power loss. It was a light loss.

Suddenly the light did, indeed, return. I rubbed my eyes and blinked. Glancing across the table, I saw that my mother was white with fear. The television was on again, the blue woman back in place. "If you can go outside, please do so," she said.

I don't like to go outside; the air is too dirty, and it hurts my lungs. Also, it reminds me of how my father died. But Mom and I went anyway, as did most of the people in our development. We had taken only a few steps outside the door when Mom looked up and gasped. I looked up, too. The gray sky was nearly blotted out by a fleet of enormous red ships. They hovered above us, not moving, as if suspended by invisible cables.

"This is the Lyran Starfleet," boomed the voice, which now seemed to come directly from the sky. "It comes in peace."

If you come in peace, why are there so many of you? I wondered.

Some people were crying, some screaming. The man next to me crossed himself, and the man next to him fainted. I felt Mom's hand tighten on my shoulder.

"Please do not panic," said the voice, its tone warm and soothing. "Now that you know our numbers, go back to your homes. We have wonders to show you."

Slowly people drifted inside. My mother leaned against me as we walked back to our door. The way she was trembling made me angry at the aliens.

When we were back in the kitchen I saw that the television was showing pictures of the Lyran Starfleet. A news announcer came on, looking terrified. "The reports we are seeing indicate that the spaceships which have suddenly appeared in our skies are so numerous they can be seen from every spot on the planet. The president has said—"

The screen blinked and the announcer disappeared. The blue-skinned woman took his place. "Please forgive us if we have frightened you," she said with a smile. "But you must understand our power before you can understand our offer."

"What does she mean?" whispered my mother.

Before I could answer—I really didn't have any idea what to say, anyway—the picture changed.

A beautiful world appeared on the screen.

"This is our home," said the alien woman. "We love it very much."

The screen showed image after image of clean cities, happy people, pristine forests. No one looked hungry. No one seemed sick.

"Now," said the woman, "let me tell you why we are here. You have many troubles. War . . . poverty . . . hunger . . . terrorism."

As she spoke, more images flowed across the screen, ugly ones: men and women, some of them much younger than me, dying in battle; children lying on dusty streets, their bellies swollen with hunger; bombs exploding among rushing crowds; a forest, yellow and dying; a dead river, thick with sludge; the remains of Chicago.

I had seen all this before, of course. But now I felt my cheeks grow hot with shame. I didn't like having visitors from another world know about these things. And I was embarrassed because I knew we should have done more to fix them.

"Do not feel bad," said the Lyran woman, as if she were reading my mind. "Once we had these problems, too. But we have solved them. That is why we have come here: to offer you our solutions."

Her face appeared on the screen again, smiling and gentle. "Think of it," she said softly. "With our help you can end war, hunger, and disease. We have cures for the mind and the body that can take you to a golden age."

"But what do they want in return?" whispered my mother. She was looking right at me, as if I would have the answer.

I shook my head. I didn't know.

"If you wish," continued the Lyran, "we will leave and let you deal with these problems on your own, as we did. But you must understand that you may not survive the process. Your world has reached a danger point, and you may destroy the planet before you heal yourselves. Or, if the majority of you prefer, we will stay and teach you what we know. But you must also understand that the knowledge we have to offer carries its own dangers. We will be providing you with tools and technology far greater than any you now possess. If we simply handed them over to you, we have little doubt that you would destroy yourselves within ten years.

"So here is what we propose: In return for our gifts, we ask you to put yourselves in our hands and let *us* care for your world until you are ready to do the job properly. You will have to give up making your own laws, of course. We will do that for you. We will run your schools. We will decide what your factories make. We will distribute the products.

"If you agree, we will give you amazing new tools. We will clean your water and take the poison from your air. We will feed your hungry, clothe your poor, heal your sick."

She smiled. "Of course, you could do these things yourselves, if you wanted to badly enough. But then, you already know that, don't you?"

The Lyran stopped smiling. "The choice you face is too important to be made by your politicians. It must be made by the people—all the people." She paused, then added, "This, too, we can make possible.

"Soon, you will fall into a deep sleep. After you do, we will prepare you for the vote. Once that is done, we will leave, so that you can think about our offer. In eight days, we will return. Then it will be time for you to vote. If you reject our offer, we will leave in peace. If you choose to accept, we will begin work immediately."

Her voice was kind. Even so, I began to shake as I felt myself grow sleepy. My mother reached out and grabbed my hand.

A moment later we were both sound asleep.

———

When I woke, my palm was itching. Without thinking, I began to scratch it. I felt something strange. Opening my hand to look, I cried out in shock. A strip of blue material stretched across the center of my palm. I ran my finger over it. Though the material was slightly raised, I could find no edge of any kind. It felt like part of my skin, almost as if it had grown there. I raised my hand to look at it more closely. The blue strip was about half an inch wide and an inch long. At each end was a black circle about the size of my fingertip.

Inside one circle was the word YES.

Inside the other it said NO.

Mom woke a few seconds later. She totally freaked when she saw the strip in her hand, of course.

When I finally got her calmed down we walked outside.

The sky was empty.

The Lyrans had gone.

"Do you believe them, Johnny?"

"I don't know, Mom. I don't know what to believe."

Other people were coming out of their homes. Everyone was talking. Fights broke out—first with words, then with fists. For some weird reason I was glad the Lyrans had gone. It was embarrassing to think of them seeing this.

When we went back inside the president was on television, making a speech about what the country would do to put an end to the alien menace. But it was just words. The Lyrans were too powerful for us. I knew it. The president knew it. Everyone knew it.

Besides, it wasn't clear they *were* a menace. After all, with their advanced science they could simply have taken over. But they hadn't.

So maybe the choice really was up to us.

I looked at my hand and began to laugh.

"What's so funny, Johnny?"

Holding my open palm in front of my mother's face, I said, "The Lyrans have made a joke. For the first time in history, our future really is in our own hands!"

JULY 23

Mom and I went to the town hall today. It was jammed with hundreds of people who had come to talk about the Lyran Proposal.

"I was in the last war!" shouted a man. "I fought to protect our freedom. I didn't want other people making choices for me then, and I don't want it now. I say no to the Lyrans!"

"I was in the same war," said a tall woman. "I saw men and women lose their legs, their arms, their eyes. I saw children with the skin burned off their bodies. We don't need another one. I say yes!"

"They'll make us slaves!" yelled someone behind me.

"They could do that without a vote," cried someone else.

Other people began shouting, until the place was ringing with voices. It took several minutes for the mayor to bring the meeting back to order.

"Look at us," said another man, once things had settled down. "We aren't hungry or poor. Most of us live long, healthy lives. Why should we vote to give control to the Lyrans?"

But what about the others? I wondered. *What about the millions who are sick and poor and dying? Should we vote no just because we're comfortable?*

The debate went on all day. Tonight the television showed other debates from all over the country, all over the world. Everywhere, people were asking the same questions: Should we? Shouldn't we? And—the biggest question of all—what do the Lyrans really want?

It seemed hard to believe they didn't want something. The thought was so strange it was almost . . . alien. Which made sense, when you thought about it.

Demonstrations were raging in most cities, with opposing mobs, some carrying signs like NUKE THE

LYRANS! and others that said VOTE LYRAN—IT'S OUR ONLY HOPE!

JULY 27

Mom hasn't gone to work for the last two days. She says she can't see any point in it. Nothing gets done at her office. All anyone can talk about, think about, is the Lyran Proposal.

JULY 29

Last night a huge screen appeared in the center of town. According to the news, screens just like it have appeared in every city in the world, every town, every village, no matter how small, no matter how remote.

They are tally screens. Tomorrow afternoon they will record the votes of six billion people as we choose whether we will rule our own future or give control to the Lyrans in return for all they have to offer.

Some people are angry that the Lyrans are letting kids vote, too. They say this should be just for adults. Me, I think the fact that the Lyrans were able to install the voting strips only on kids over the age of ten shows how powerful they really are. And I don't see why kids, even fairly little ones, shouldn't vote. It's their world, too. It's their future, even more than the grown-ups', since they're going to be living in it longer.

Though some people say one person's vote doesn't count, I've been taking mine very seriously. My mind is spinning with all I have heard this week, all the words about the poor and the sick and the dying; about freedom and power and dignity.

I don't want aliens to run our world. But when I look around, when I see what a mess it is, I feel afraid for our future if they don't. I just don't know if we're grown-up enough to take care of ourselves. Mom and I keep arguing about this. The thing is, half the time I'm in favor of the Lyrans and she's arguing against them, and the other half of the time it's the other way around.

Last night she got out the family album and we spent a couple of hours looking at old pictures. The ones that really got to me, of course, were the photos of Dad. I can't help but think he might still be alive if we had had Lyran science six years ago.

What would he have said about all this? He was a proud man—proud and stubborn. Would he have wanted to live under someone else's rule?

Do I?

JULY 30

I am sitting in my room, staring at the strip of alien material embedded in my palm. I am thinking of all I have seen, all I have done, all I want to do.

I am thinking of the last time I saw my father, cold and still in his coffin, and how Lyran medicine might have saved him—how Lyran science might have prevented the air crisis and saved so many others like him.

I think of our glory and our despair. I think of all we do to one another in the name of love, of peace, of freedom, of God—all the good, and all the bad.

I think of how far we have come in just a few thousand years. I think of how far there is to go and how many people will suffer and die before we get there.

I think of the stars, and of the worlds out there waiting for us to join them.

I think of all these things, and I wonder what I will do in five minutes when the Lyrans force me to choose between the riches they offer and the freedom to find our own sad and starry path.

I look at the strip in my hand, at the YES and the NO, and I wonder.

What's the Worst That Could Happen?

IF THIRTEEN is supposed to be an unlucky number, what does it mean that we are forced to go through an entire year with that as our age? I mean, you would think a civilized society could just come up with a way for us to skip it.

Of course, good luck and I have rarely shared the same park bench. Sometimes I think Murphy's Law—you know, "If something can go wrong, it will"—was invented just for me.

I suppose the fact that my name is Murphy Murphy might have something to do with that feeling.

Yeah, you read it right: Murphy Murphy. It's like a family curse. The last name I got from my father, of course. The first name came down from my mother's side, where it is a tradition for the firstborn son. You

would think my mother might have considered that before she married Dad, but love makes fools of us all, I
guess. Anyway, the fact that I got stuck with the same
name coming and going, so to speak, shows that my parents are either spineless (my theory) or have no common
sense (my sister's theory).

I would like to note that no one has ever apologized
to me for this name. "I think it's lovely," says my
mother—which, when you consider it, would seem to
support my sister's theory.

Anyway, you can see that right from the beginning of
my life, if something could go wrong, it did.

Okay, I suppose it could have been worse. I could
have been born dead or with two heads or something.
On the other hand, as I lie here in my hospital bed trying to work out exactly how I got here, there are times
when I wonder if being born dead might not have been
the best thing.

To begin with, I want to say here and now that
Mikey Farnsworth should take at least part of the blame
for this situation. This, by the way, is true for many of the
bad things that have happened in my life, from the paste-
eating incident in first grade through the bogus fire-drill
situation last year, right up to yesterday afternoon, which
was sort of the Olympics of Bad Luck, as far as I'm con-

cerned. What's amazing is that somehow Mikey ends up coming out of these things looking perfectly fine. He is, as my grandfather likes to say, the kind of guy who can fall in a manure pile and come out smelling like a rose.

The one I am not going to blame is Tiffany Grimsley, though if I hadn't had this stupid crush on her it never would have happened.

Okay, I want to stop and talk about this whole thing of having a crush. Let me say right up front that it is very confusing and not something I am used to. When it started I was totally baffled. I mean, I don't even like girls, and all of a sudden I keep thinking about one of them? Give me a break!

In case it hasn't happened to you yet, let me warn you. Based on personal experience, I can say that while there are many bad things about having a crush, just about the worst of them is the stupid things you will do because of it.

Okay, let's back up here.

I probably wouldn't even have known I had a crush to begin with if Mikey hadn't informed me of this fact. "Man, you've got it bad for Tiffany," he says one day when we are poking around in the swamp behind his house.

"What are you talking about?" I ask. At the same time

my cheeks begin to burn as if they are on fire. Startled, I lift my foot to tie my shoe, which is a trick I learned in an exercise magazine and that has become sort of a habit. At the moment, it is mostly an excuse to look down.

What the heck is going on here? I think.

Mikey laughs. "Look at you blush, Murphy! There's no point in trying to hide it. I watched you drooling over her in social studies class today. And you've only mentioned her like sixteen times since we got home this afternoon."

"Well, sure, but that's because she's a friend," I say, desperately trying to avoid the horrible truth. "We've known each other since kindergarten, for pete's sake."

Mikey laughs again, and I can tell I'm not fooling him. "What am I going to do?" I groan.

He shrugs. "Either you suffer in silence or you tell her you like her."

Is he nuts? If you tell a girl you like her, it puts you totally out in the open. I mean, you've got no place to hide. And there are really only two possible responses you're going to get from her: (a) She likes you, too, which the more you think about it, the more unlikely it seems or (b) anything else, which is, like, totally, utterly humiliating. I'm sure girls have problems of their own. But I don't think they have any idea of the sheer terror a guy has to go through before any boy-girl stuff can get started.

I sure hope this gets easier with time, because I personally really don't understand how the human race has managed to survive this long, given how horrifying it is to think about telling a girl you like her.

Despite Mikey's accusation, I do not think I have actually drooled over Tiffany during social studies class. But it is hard not to think about her then, because she sits right in front of me. It's the last class of the day, and the October sunlight comes in slantwise and catches in her golden hair in a way that makes it hard to breathe.

It does not help that eighth-grade social studies is taught by Herman Fessenden, who you will probably see on the front of the *National Enquirer* someday as a mass murderer for boring twenty-six kids to death in a single afternoon. It hasn't happened yet, but I'm sure it's just a matter of time.

I spend the entire weekend thinking about what Mikey has said, and I come up with a bold plan, which is to pass Tiffany a note asking if she wants to grab a slice of pizza at Angelo's after school. I am just getting up my nerve to do it—there are only five minutes of class left—when Mr. F. says, "So, what do you think the queen should have done then, Murphy?"

How am I supposed to know? But I blush and don't hand the note to Tiffany after all, which wouldn't have been so bad, except that Butch Coulter sees I have it and grabs it on the way out of class, and I have to give him the rest of my week's lunch money to get it back.

Tuesday I try a new tactic. There's a little store on the way to school where you can pick up candy and gum and stuff, and I get some on the way to school, and then kind of poke Tiff in the back during social studies class, which is about the only time I see her, to ask if she wants a piece of gum. Only before she can answer, Mr. Fessenden comes up from behind and snatches the whole pack out of my hand. So that was that.

Then, on Wednesday, it's as if the gods are smiling on me, which is not something I am used to. Tiffany grabs my arm on the way out of social studies and says, "Can I talk to you for a second, Murphy?"

"Sure," I say. This is not very eloquent, but it is better than the first thought that crosses my mind, which is, "Any time, any where, any moment of the day." It is also better than "Your words would be like nectar flowing into the hungry mouths of my ears," which was a line I had come up with for a poem I was writing about her.

She actually looks a little shy, though what this

goddess-on-earth has to be shy about is more than I can imagine.

She hands me a folded-over set of papers, and my heart skips a beat. Can this be a love letter? If so, it's a really long one.

"I wrote this skit for drama club, and I thought maybe you would do it with me next Friday. I think you'd be just right for the part."

My heart starts pounding. While it seems unlikely that the part is that of a barbarian warrior prince, just doing it means I will have an excuse to spend time with Tiffany. I mean, we'll have to rehearse and . . . well, the imagination staggers.

"Yes!" I say, ignoring the facts that (a) I have not yet read the script and (b) I have paralyzing stage fright.

She gives me one of those sunrise smiles of hers, grabs my arm and gives it a squeeze, and says, "Thanks. This is going to be fun." Then she's gone, leaving me with a memory of her fingers on my arm and a wish that I had started pumping iron when I was in first grade, so my biceps would have been ready for this moment.

Mikey moves in a second later. "Whoa," he says, nudging me with his elbow. "Progress! What did she say?"

"She wants me to do a skit with her."

He shakes his head. "Too bad. I thought maybe you had a chance. How'd she take it when you told her no?"

I look at him in surprise. "I didn't. I said I would do it."

Mikey looks even more surprised. "Murphy, you can't go on stage with her. You can't even move when you get on stage. Don't you remember what happened in fifth grade?"

As if I could forget. Not only was it one of the three most humiliating moments of my life, but according to my little brother it has become legendary at Westcott Elementary. Here's the short version: Mrs. Carmichael had cast me as George Washington in our class play, and I was, I want to tell you, pretty good during rehearsals. But when they opened the curtain and I saw the audience . . . well, let's just say that when my mother saw the look on my face she actually let out a scream. She told me later she thought I was having a heart attack. As for me, my mouth went drier than day-old toast, some mysterious object wedged itself in my throat, and the only reason I didn't bolt from the stage was that I couldn't move my arms or legs. Heck, I couldn't even move my fingers.

I couldn't even squeak!

Finally they had to cancel the performance. Even after the curtains were closed it took two teachers and a janitor to carry me back to the classroom.

"This time will be different," I say.

Mikey snorts.

I know he is right. "Oh man, what am I gonna do?" I wail.

"Come on, let's look at the script. Maybe all you have to do is sit there and she'll do all the acting."

No such luck. The script, which is called *Debbie and the Doofus,* is very funny.

It also calls for me to say a lot of lines.

It also calls for me to act like a complete dork.

Immediately I begin to wonder why Tiffany thinks I would be just right for this role.

"Maybe she imagines you're a brilliant actor," says Mikey.

He is trying to be helpful, but to tell the truth, I am not sure which idea is worse: that Tiffany thinks I am a dork, or that she thinks I am a brilliant actor.

"What am I gonna do?" I wail again.

"Maybe your parents will move before next week," says Mikey, shaking his head. "Otherwise, you're a dead man walking."

I ask, but my parents are not planning on moving.

I study the script as if it is the final exam for life, which as far as I am concerned, it is. After two days I know not only my lines but all of Tiffany's lines, too, as well as the lines for Laurel Gibbon, who is going to be playing the waitress at the little restaurant where we go for our bad date.

My new plan is that I will enjoy rehearsals, and the excuse they give me to be with Tiffany, then pray for a meteor to strike me before the day of the performance.

The first half of this actually seems to work. We have two rehearsals, one at school, and one in Tiffany's rec room. At the first one she is very impressed by the fact that I know my lines already. "This is great, Murphy!" she says, which makes me feel as if I have won the lottery.

At the second rehearsal I actually make Laurel, who is perhaps the most solemn girl in the school, laugh. This is an amazing sound to me, and I find that I really enjoy it. Like Tiffany, Laurel has been in our class since kindergarten. Only I never noticed her much because, well, no one ever notices Laurel much, on account of she basically doesn't talk. I wondered at first why Tiffany had cast her, but it turns out they are in the same church group and have been good friends for a long time.

Sometimes I think the girls in our class have a whole secret life that I don't know about.

———

Time becomes very weird. Sometimes it seems as if the hours are rushing by in a blur, the moment of performance hurtling toward me. Other times the clock seems to poke along like a sloth with chronic fatigue syndrome. Social studies class consists of almost nothing but staring at the sunshine in Tiffany's hair and flubbing the occasional question that Mr. Fessenden lobs at me. Some days I think he asks me questions out of pure meanness. Other days he leaves me alone, and I almost get the impression he feels sorry for me.

Mikey and I talk about the situation every night. "No meteor yet," he'll say, shaking his head.

"What am I gonna do?" I reply, repeating the question that haunts my days. I can't possibly tell Tiffany I can't do this.

"Maybe you could be sick that day?" says Mikey.

I shake my head. "If I let her down I will hate myself forever."

Mikey rolls his eyes. "Maybe you should run away from home," he suggests, not very helpfully.

Finally we do come up with a plan, which is that Mikey will stay in the wings to prompt me in case the entire script falls out of my head. I don't know if this will really do much good, since if I freeze with terror, mere prompting will not be of much use. On the other hand, knowing Mikey will be there calms me down a little. It's like having a life jacket.

Hah! Little do I know what kind of life jacket he will turn out to be.

To my dismay, I have not been able to parlay my time working on the skit with Tiffany into anything bigger. This is partly because she is the busiest person in the eighth grade, with more clubs and committees and activities than any normal person could ever be involved with. It is also because I am stupid about this kind of thing and don't have the slightest clue how to do it. So I treasure my memory of the two rehearsals and, more than anything else, the sound of her laughing at some of what I have done.

Despite my prayers, Friday arrives. I don't suppose I really expected God to cancel it, though I would have been deeply appreciative if he had. I go through the day in a state of cold terror. The drama club meeting is after school. Members of the club have invited their friends, their families, and some teachers to come see the skits. There are going to be four skits in all. Tiffany, Laurel, and I are scheduled to go last, which gives me more time to sweat and worry.

Mikey is backstage with us, but Tiffany does not know why. I tell her he came because he is my pal. Getting him aside, I check to make sure he has the script.

At 2:45, Mrs. Whitcomb, the drama club coach, comes back to wish us luck. She makes a little speech, which she ends with, "Okay, kids, break a leg!"

This, of course, is how people wish each other luck in the theater. According to my mother, the idea is that you're not going to get your wish anyway, so you wish for the thing you don't want, and you may get the thing you do want instead.

I suddenly wonder if this is what I have been doing wrong all my life.

On the other hand, Tiffany is standing next to me, so that is one wish that is continuing to come true.

"Are you excited?" she asks.

"You have no idea," I answer, with complete honesty.

Laurel, who is standing on the other side of me, whispers, "I'm scared."

"Don't worry, you'll be fine," I reply.

I am fairly confident this is true, since I expect to make such an ass of myself that no one will notice anything else, anyway. Inside me, a small voice is screaming, *What were you thinking of, you moron? You are going to humiliate yourself in front of all these people, including the girl you*

*would cut out your heart for, who will be even more humiliated
than you are, because it's her skit that you are messing up! Run
away! Run away!*

If I could get my hands on this small voice I would
gladly beat it to a bloody pulp. Instead I keep taking deep
breaths and reminding myself how funny I was during
the second rehearsal.

The first skit goes up. I think it's funny, but at first
people don't laugh. This terrifies me all over again. Then
someone snickers. A moment later someone else lets out
a snort. Pretty soon people are enjoying themselves.
Clearly it takes people a while to get warmed up when
they are trying to have fun.

At first the sound of that laughter is soothing. People
are ready to have a good time. But it takes only a few
minutes for me to get terrified by it. What if they don't
laugh at our skit? Even worse, what if they laugh for the
wrong reasons? What if Tiffany is totally humiliated and
it's all my fault?

I go back to wanting to die.

The second skit goes up, and dies in my place. It just
lies onstage, stinking the place up like a week-old fish.
It's as boring as last month's news. In fact, it's almost
as boring as Mr. Fessenden, which I would not have

thought possible. I feel a surge of hope. We can't possibly look worse than this. In fact, next to it we'll seem like geniuses. Too bad we can't go on right away!

Unfortunately, we have to wait for the third skit, which turns out to be brilliant, which makes me want to kill the people who are in it. Now we'll be compared to them instead of the dead fish of that second skit.

The curtain closes.

"Our turn," whispers Tiffany. "Break a leg, Murphy."

"Break a leg," I murmur back. Then, so Laurel won't feel left out, I say the same thing to her as we pick up the table, which is our main prop, and move it onto the stage. Tiffany is right behind us with a pair of chairs. Once they're in place, we scurry to our positions, Tiffany and me stage right, Laurel stage left.

My stomach clenches. Cold sweat starts out on my brow.

"Murphy!" hisses Tiffany. "Your shoelace!"

I glance down. I have forgotten to untie it, which is the key to one of my first funny bits. Out of habit, I lift my foot to take care of the lace. At that instant the curtain opens, which startles me so much that I lose my balance and fall over, landing onstage in full view of the audience.

There they are. The enemy. The people who are going to stare at me, judge me, whisper about me tomorrow. I am so frozen with terror I cannot move. I just lie there looking at them.

And then the laugh begins. My temperature goes in two directions, my blood turning to ice at the same time that the heat rises in my face. I have a long moment of terror—well, it feels like a long moment; according to Mikey, it was less than two seconds—while I think that this is it, I will never stand up again, never come to school again, never leave my house again. I will ask whoever finally picks me up to carry me home and put me in the attic. My parents will have to shove my meals through a slot in the door, because I will never be able to face another living human being.

Love saves the day. "Murphy, are you all right?" hisses Tiffany.

For the sound of that voice I would do anything— even get back on my feet.

And then, the second miracle. Some brilliant portion of my brain realizes that this is a comedy, and I have just started us off with a big laugh. I stand at the edge of the stage to do a fake knock. In rehearsal, I only mimed it. Now, for some reason, I say loudly, *"Knock knock. Knockity-knock-knock."*

For some reason the audience finds this funny. Another laugh.

Tiffany comes to the door, and we go through our opening business, which establishes that she is prim and proper and I am a total idiot, which doesn't take much acting because it is pretty much real life anyway. But something is happening. I'm not making up lines, but I am making bigger gestures, broader moves, weirder voices than I did in rehearsal. People are howling. Tiffany's eyes are dancing, and I can see that she is trying not to laugh. I am feeling like a genius.

We get to the imaginary restaurant. Laurel comes out to take our order, and I have the same effect on her.

I am starting to feel as if I'm having an out-of-body experience. Who is this funny person making everyone laugh? How long can it go on? Can I keep it going, keep cranking up the jokes, hold on to this glorious lightning bolt I'm riding?

Laurel disappears to get our order. I fake blowing my nose on the cloth napkin, then inspecting it to see the results. I act as if I am fascinated by my imaginary boogers. Tiffany acts as if she is repulsed, but I can see she is hardly able to keep from bursting into laughter— especially when I hand the napkin across the table so she can examine it, too.

The audience is just about screaming. I am beginning to think that this kind of laughter is even better than the sound of Tiffany's voice.

Laurel comes back with our "order," which, because this is a skit and we are on a low budget, is a plate of Hostess cupcakes. Chocolate.

I am supposed to eat in a disgusting way. The script does not specify how. Still riding my wave of improvisation inspiration, I pick up a cupcake and stuff the entire thing into my mouth. Tiffany's eyes widen and she turns her head to hide the laugh she can't hold in. Her shoulders are shaking. This is too good to be true.

I deliver my next line—which is about how beautiful she is—with bits of chocolate spewing out. It's disgusting, but hilarious. Tiffany has tears streaming down her cheeks from trying to hold in her laughter.

Desperate to keep the riff going, I cram another entire cupcake into my mouth.

This is when disaster strikes. Suddenly I discover that I can't breathe, because there is a chocolate logjam in my throat. I only need a minute, I think, and I'll get this. I try to give my next line, but nothing comes out. Tiffany starts to look alarmed. The audience is still laughing, but it's starting to die down, as if some of them realize I am in trouble.

Which is when Mikey comes barreling onstage from behind me, screaming, "He's choking! He's choking!"

He grabs me around the waist and jabs his fists into my belly.

I've been Heimliched!

Those of you who know about the Heimlich maneuver will remember that basically it forces the air out of your lungs, blowing whatever is blocking your breathing out of your mouth.

Those of you who have been staging this in your mind as you read will remember who is directly across from me.

Those of you with even minimal powers of prediction will know what happens next. An unholy mix of partially chewed Hostess chocolate cupcakes spews out of my mouth and spatters all over Tiffany.

I am filled with deeper horror than any I have ever known. Wrenching my way out of Mikey's grasp, I bolt around the table to clean her off.

Unfortunately, the table is close to the edge of the stage. Too close. Tripping over my untied shoelace, I hurtle headfirst into the darkness.

My body makes some very unpleasant sounds as it lands.

———

Okay, I probably could have accepted the broken leg.

I might even have been able to live with the memory of the look on Tiffany's face.

But when the ambulance guys came and put me on a stretcher, and everyone stood there watching as they rolled me out of the school, and Mikey followed after them to tell me that my fly had been open during the entire fiasco, I really thought that was too much.

Anyway, that's how I ended up in this hospital bed, staring at my right leg, which is up in traction.

Tiffany came to visit a while ago. That would have been wonderful, except she brought along her boyfriend, Chuck. He goes to another school and is old enough to drive.

Something inside me died when she introduced him.

To make things worse (and what doesn't?), it turns out that Chuck was in the audience yesterday.

"You were brilliant, man," he says. "At least, until the part where it all fell to pieces."

I want to shove a Hostess cupcake down his throat.

After they are gone, Mikey shows up.

"Tough luck, Murphy," he says, looking at my cast.

I try to remember that he is my best friend, and really thought he was saving my life when he Heimliched me.

It is not easy.

"Cheer up," he says. "It couldn't get worse than this."

He's lucky my leg is in traction and I can't get out of bed. He is also lucky I don't have a cupcake on me.

After Mikey leaves, I make two decisions: (a) I am going to change my name, and (b) I never want to be thirteen again as long as I live.

There is another knock on my door.

"Hello, Murphy," says a soft voice.

It's Laurel.

She smiles shyly. "Can I come in?"

I've never noticed how pretty she is when she smiles. For a brief moment I think life may not be so bad after all.

I am pretty sure, however, that this is a delusion.

After all, my name is still Murphy Murphy.

And I'm still thirteen years old.

I don't even want to think about what might happen next.

The Ghost Let Go

THUNDER rumbled overhead.

A crack of lightning split the midnight sky.

My father said a word I don't get to use.

"What's the matter, James?" asked Chris Gurley. (My father's name is actually Henry, but Chris and I were sitting in the backseat and pretending he was our chauffeur, so we were calling him James.)

"Nothing," Dad muttered, as heavy drops began to spatter the windshield. "I just wanted to get back to Syracuse before this storm started. I'm exhausted."

We were driving home from a Halloween storytelling concert put on by a couple of Dad's friends. I was thinking about their last story, the tale of "The Phantom Hitchhiker," when I spotted a woman walking along the road ahead of us.

I felt a shiver, as if the story was coming true. *Stop it, Nine,* I told myself. *You're being silly.* Before I could suggest to Dad that we should offer the woman a ride she turned and ran straight at us, waving her arms wildly. As she got closer I could see that she was screaming. For a terrifying moment, I actually thought she was going to fling herself onto our hood.

"Dad, watch out!" I cried—unnecessarily, since he was already slamming his foot against the brake and wrenching the steering wheel to the right. I caught a terrifying glimpse of the woman's twisted, screaming face through my window as we shot past, missing her by inches.

We were going way too fast when we hit the side of the road. Next thing I knew we were bouncing down a steep bank, and I realized with horror that we were going to roll over.

Everything seemed to slow down as the car went onto its side, then its top. When we stopped, I was hanging upside down in the dark, held in place by my seat belt. The radio had somehow gotten turned on, and a country-and-western song was blaring through the dark, which only added to the weirdness.

"Nine!" cried my father, shouting to be heard above the radio. "Chris! Are you all right?"

"I think so," muttered Chris. I could tell from the sound of her voice that she was also upside down.

"I'm all right," I said. "Except for the blood rushing to my head."

I noticed that my voice was shaking.

"See if you can unhook your seat belts," said Dad.

I reached down with my hand. The car roof—which was now the floor—was only a couple of inches from my skull. Bracing myself, I fiddled with the seat belt. When I finally opened the buckle I fell to the ceiling, landing on my head.

I heard a thump as Chris landed beside me. Between the music, the darkness, the hanging upside down, and the terror of the accident, we were pretty confused. It took a few moments of crawling around on the ceiling/floor to find one of the doors, and a few more to pry it open.

The rain was coming down so hard that within seconds my clothes were soaked and clinging to my skin. I was so relieved to be out of the car that I didn't really care.

Once we had finished checking to see if we really were all okay, my father muttered, "I'd like to get my hands on that dame. Do you think that was some sort of Halloween prank, or is she merely crazy?" He stopped as if struck by what he had just said and looked around nervously, obviously wondering if a crazy woman might be watching us even now.

"Where do you suppose she went, anyway?" asked Chris, sounding as nervous as I felt.

I looked around, but between the darkness and the rain, I doubt I would have seen her if she was standing more than ten feet away.

"You two keep your eyes open," ordered Dad. Then he turned his attention to the car.

"How bad is it, Mr. T.?" asked Chris after a minute.

"I won't know until we can get a better look at it," he said mournfully.

I felt really bad for him. The Golden Chariot, as he calls our car, is a 1959 Cadillac. It's huge (comparing it to a modern car is like comparing a seven-layer cake to an Oreo) and it's my father's pride and joy. He's a preservation architect, after all, and he likes his cars the way he likes his buildings—big, old, and fancy. Given the time and money he had put into the Chariot, I could see why he would feel bitter toward the woman who caused us to plunge into the ditch.

Despite her spooky appearance, it didn't occur to me to think the woman might have been a ghost. After all,

Dad had seen her, too, and while by this time in our lives Chris and I had seen several ghosts, Dad had yet to spot one. It just wasn't something you expected of him.

"Well, we can't stand out here in the rain," he said gloomily. "We'd better see if we can find someplace where we can make a few phone calls."

"That may not be easy," said Chris.

She was right. We had been taking one of my father's famous "shortcuts" along an old country road and hadn't seen a house for the last two miles. Which meant we could either walk back those two miles through the pounding rain, or keep going on the hope that we might find a house not far ahead. Since we couldn't really get any wetter even if we tried, we decided to gamble on going forward.

"Besides," said Dad, "maybe we'll run into that maniac and I can give her a piece of my mind. Wait a minute while I get the flashlight."

Lying on his back, he managed to retrieve a flashlight from the glove compartment. Following his lead, we scrambled out of the ditch and up to the road. The rain was pelting down so hard that it hurt. Since there was pretty much zero traffic, we were soon walking side by side. I kept looking around, worrying that the woman might jump out of the bushes or something. What she had done already was so crazy there was no telling what else she might do.

Here's the first thing I learned that night: If you walk through freezing rain for twenty minutes, you'll probably be willing to knock on the door of a house you normally wouldn't get near on a bet—especially if there's no other house in sight. Of course, given how dark it was, "in sight" didn't amount to much in this case.

Actually, we didn't even see the house at first. We only realized it was there because I bumped into something and shouted "Ouch!" When Dad lifted the beam of the flashlight to see what the problem was, we saw a mailbox. The name B. SMILEY was painted on the side.

"They've got to be kidding," snorted Chris.

"I don't care if Smiley shares the house with Dopey, Doc, and Grumpy," I replied, "as long as they let us out of this rain."

Though the house wasn't visible from the road, we found an unpaved driveway just past the mailbox. It was lined with trees whose branches met overhead, making it almost a tunnel. The branches provided a little relief from the storm, but the effect was so creepy I decided I would have preferred the rain.

Just before we left the tree tunnel a bolt of lightning

revealed the house. It was about fifty feet ahead of us. Tall and brooding, it had a steep roof and a pair of spooky gables. It looked like something out of a nightmare, the kind of place you're *supposed* to find when your car breaks down on a cold, rainy night. The only light came from a single window on the second floor.

My father waited until the rumble of thunder had passed, then said, "Well . . . is it?"

What he meant was, "Is it haunted?"

This wasn't an unreasonable question. Ever since Chris and I had met the Woman in White at the Grand Theater, we had been growing increasingly sensitive to ghosts. Sometimes we knew if a place was haunted just by looking at it.

Sometimes, but not always.

"I can't tell," replied Chris, shouting to be heard above the sudden gust of wind that made the shutters on the house begin to bang.

"Me, either!" I bellowed.

I didn't bother to add that I had come to the conclusion that people were a lot more dangerous than ghosts anyway. Not that I don't find ghosts eerie. Something about meeting the spirit of a person who has crossed into the world of the dead makes my flesh tingle no matter how many times it happens.

"Well, standing in the rain is stupid," said Dad at last. "Let's go."

Leaving the cover of the trees, he sprinted toward the porch. I don't know why he bothered to run; we were already totally drenched. Maybe it was the promise of shelter being so close. Pointless or not, Chris and I sprinted after him.

The steps sagged beneath our weight as we dashed up to the porch. It was a relief to be out of the downpour— even if it meant standing at the threshold of such a weird-looking place.

Dad stared at the door for a moment but didn't make any move to summon the owner. "Don't be silly, Henry," he muttered to himself at last. "It's just an old house in the country." He played the beam of the flashlight over the doorframe until he found the doorbell button. He pushed it vigorously.

No one answered for a long time. I was wondering if we were going to have to start walking again when an old man's face appeared at the little window in the door. His expression was hard to read, and at first I thought he was going to turn around and leave us standing on the porch. But after a moment the door creaked open.

"Can I help you?" he asked.

His voice was scratchy, as if he didn't use it very often.

"We had an accident up the road a bit," said my father. "Could we use your phone, please?"

A strange expression flickered across the old man's face. It vanished almost immediately, as if he had caught himself telling a secret. His features froze into place, only his eyes betraying that something bothered him. With a shake of his head he said, "Don't have a phone."

My father sighed. He tried to keep it from showing, but I could tell from his eyes he was feeling a little desperate. "Is there anyone near here who *does* have a phone?" he asked.

The old man shook his head again, and I noticed that he was wearing a hearing aid. "No one near here at all," he said.

"Any chance you could give us a ride?" asked Dad. He was sounding more desperate with each question.

Another shake of the head. "I don't drive anymore."

Dad looked back at the storm. He took a deep breath, then said, "I know it's a lot to ask, but could we possibly stay here for the night?"

It was the old man's turn to hesitate. He studied the three of us for a moment, then nodded and stepped aside so that we could enter.

His silence was spooky, but not as spooky as his house. The place looked like something from another time—or at least as if it hadn't been cleaned since some earlier period in history. Dust lay thick on every surface. Cobwebs tangled in the corners. The pattern on the carpet had nearly disappeared.

"My name is Henry Tanleven," said my father, extending his hand.

The old man looked at my father's hand as if he wasn't sure what he was supposed to do with it. Finally he took it in his own and said, "Benjamin Smiley."

"Pleased to meet you, Mr. Smiley," said my father. "And my apologies for intruding on you this way. This is my daughter, Nine, and her friend, Chris Gurley."

Mr. Smiley looked surprised by my name. "It's really Nina," I explained, as I did almost every time I first met someone. "People call me Nine because they like the way it sounds when you put it together with my last name."

Usually people take a second to figure out the joke, then smile and nod. Sometimes they start to smile before I explain, because they've already figured it out. Despite his name, Mr. Smiley looked as if he had no idea what a joke was. He just stared at me and said "Nine" in a flat voice.

Before I could think of what to say, an enormous clap of thunder shook the walls of the house.

The lights went out.

A terrifying screech ripped through the darkness.

I shouted and reached for Chris. She was trying to grab me as well, and for a weird moment we sort of clawed at each other.

"Shut up!" yelled Mr. Smiley.

Was he yelling at us or whoever had made the screech? If the latter, it didn't work, because the same voice shrieked, "Lights! Turn on the lights!"

"Stupid bird," muttered Mr. Smiley.

"Bird?" I asked in a small voice.

"It's my parrot, Commander Cody," he said in disgust. "He tends to get excited when the weather is rough."

At that moment the lights came back on.

"Thank you!" squawked the bird.

I felt a little safer. The bird was weird, but it was a normal kind of weird, if you know what I mean. Which was more than I could say for Benjamin Smiley. An air of deep sadness seemed to cling to him, and I felt that simply by knocking at his door we had done something incredibly intrusive.

"Come along," he said. "I'll show you where you can sleep."

"Jeremiah!" squawked the bird, as we started up the stairway. "Go to Jeremiah!"

We followed Mr. Smiley along a hallway where the pink and gray wallpaper had started to peel but was refusing to let go altogether. "You two can stay in here," he said, opening the door to a room that smelled dank and musty. He waved his hand to the right. "The bathroom is down the hall."

He flipped a switch, turning on a single bare bulb that hung from the ceiling. The bed itself, covered with a worn, pink chenille spread, was old and sagging. Given the circumstances, it was one of the most beautiful things I had ever seen.

"I'm glad we had already arranged for you to stay overnight with us," my father said to Chris. "At least your parents won't be worried about where you are."

"My parents always worry when I go someplace with Nine," replied Chris.

My father rolled his eyes. Turning to Mr. Smiley, he said, "I don't mind sleeping on a couch. I feel terrible troubling you like this."

"No need for that," said the old man gruffly. "You can use the room across the hall."

As soon as they were gone Chris closed the door and said, "This whole thing is fishier than Mrs. Paul's kitchen. Something very weird is going on here."

"I agree. Only I can't put my finger on anything specific. I mean, it's a little odd for the old guy to be living out here all alone, but lots of people are sort of odd. It just feels like there's something more . . ."

"Didn't you recognize what happened to us out there?" she asked. "It was just like the last story we heard, the one about the phantom hitchhiker."

I shivered. "I was thinking about that one just before we had the accident," I admitted.

You probably know the story. A man is driving down a country road late at night and picks up a young female hitchhiker. Later—after the girl has either gotten out of the car or vanished, sometimes after asking him to deliver a message—he stops and has to stay with some people along the road. The man either describes the hitchhiker to his hosts, or spots her picture on the mantelpiece. A terrible look comes over their faces, and they tell him that his passenger was their daughter, who had died in a horrible car crash many years earlier.

I saw a couple of problems in matching that story up with what we had just experienced. For one thing, the woman we saw hadn't been hitchhiking.

Chris nodded when I pointed this out. "But remember, in the story it's always a man traveling *alone* who spots the ghost. So maybe the fact that *we* were in the car kept her from trying to catch a ride."

"Also, we didn't spot anyone's picture on the mantel."

"No, but did you notice the look on Mr. Smiley's face when your father said we had had an accident? I bet he's heard *that* before!"

"So what are you saying? That we're trapped in the classic American ghost story?"

"I don't know *what* I'm saying, except that there's something weird going on around here."

I looked around the room. It was oddly bare. The only furniture besides the bed and nightstand was a low dresser with two items on top of it: a small lamp and a big, old family Bible. I started to examine the Bible, but Chris called me to the closet instead. "Take a look at this!" she whispered.

I went to stand beside her. The closet was filled with women's clothes, all of them old-fashioned.

Before I could think of what to say, we heard a knock at the door. Quickly, Chris closed the closet.

"Who's there?" I called.

"It's me," said Mr. Smiley. "I brought you some towels."

It was an unexpected kindness, and I revised my opinion of him upward a couple of notches.

We stripped and dried ourselves off, then climbed

into the old bed. It creaked and groaned underneath us, and the worn springs tended to roll us toward the middle.

"It's going to be a long night," muttered Chris after a few minutes of this.

"It already has been," I replied.

Given the night's excitement, I didn't know if I would be able to sleep or not. But exhaustion can work wonders, and it wasn't long before I nodded off.

It wasn't much longer before Chris woke me by nudging me in the ribs with her elbow. "Nine! Listen!"

I listened.

The little hairs on the back of my neck stood up.

Somewhere below us a woman was crying.

Question number one: Should we stay where we were or go investigate? The sensible thing, of course, was to stay put.

Chris and I have never been accused of being sensible.

Even so, I wasn't sure we should go wandering around in Mr. Smiley's house. "He seems like an awfully cranky old guy," I whispered to Chris when we started to discuss the matter.

"You'd be cranky, too, if you had some woman crying her eyes out downstairs every night."

"What makes you think it happens every night?"

She shrugged. "Okay, once a month. Who knows? But if that's a ghost—and I bet it is—then I also bet she does it on a regular basis."

"Maybe he doesn't even hear it," I replied. "I bet he takes out his hearing aid at night."

"And your father is so exhausted he'll probably sleep right through it, too. Which means it's up to *us* to see what's wrong."

When I still hesitated, she hit me with the argument that I can never resist: "Look, Nine, not everyone can do what we do. We have a *responsibility* to help this ghost."

What could I say? Maybe this woman had been weeping down there every night for ages, waiting for someone to help her. Maybe fate had brought Chris and me here for that very purpose.

"All right," I sighed. "We'd better go take a look."

Question number two: Should we put on our clothes? They were still wet, and cold to boot. I was willing to wander around the house without permission, but I wasn't willing to do so naked. At least, not until I started to pull on my jeans. Then I had second thoughts.

"These are freezing!" I hissed.

We briefly considered the clothes in the closet. However, we decided that since (a) they might actually belong to the ghost and (b) Mr. Smiley might catch us in them, we should leave them alone. In the end, we went for the blankets. Well, I got the blanket. Chris got the pink chenille bedspread. She wasn't entirely happy about this, but we played "Rock, Paper, Scissors" for the blanket and I won, so there wasn't much she could say.

"I feel silly," I whispered as we stepped into the hall. My teeth were still chattering, even though I was much warmer now that I was wrapped in the blanket.

"*You* feel silly!" hissed Chris. "I'm the one dressed in Donna Reed's bedspread! Come on, we have to find that woman before she disappears. You never know how long a ghost is going to hang around."

With that, she grabbed my elbow and steered me toward the stairs.

"I wish we had a flashlight," I whispered.

"Stop talking and listen," replied Chris.

The weeping was coming from right below us.

Side by side, we headed down the stairwell.

The ghost was in the living room. We knew she was a ghost because even though there was no light—not even moonlight, since the storm was still going on—we could see her clearly. She was glowing softly, as if illumined from within. We couldn't see her face—it was buried in her hands. She was sitting on the couch, leaning away from us, her shoulders shaking as if she were sobbing.

I assumed she was the woman we had seen walking in the storm. I would also have assumed that she was the one we had heard weeping, except for one thing: The sound wasn't coming from the ghost. It was coming from somewhere behind us. And since we had never heard a ghost before, I assumed whoever was making the sound must be a living person. Which left us with the next question: Should we stay and watch the ghost or go and tend to the living?

Of course, we could have split up and done both, but under the circumstances, it wasn't an idea that appealed to either of us.

The weeping was so heartbreaking that after a moment I whispered to Chris, "I think we'd better go see about that. I bet it's connected to the ghost somehow."

Taking my arm, she led the way. We moved carefully, trying not to make any noise. Even so, when I glanced over my shoulder, I saw that the ghost seemed to be fading.

A moment later we reached an open doorway that led to the kitchen—something we realized only because a tiny bulb on the top of the stove provided enough light to make out the major shapes in the room.

A woman sat at the table with her back to us. Her long hair covered her shoulders.

At the sight of her, I felt my flesh begin to crawl. The way she was holding herself—face in hands, shoulders shaking as she wept—made her look uncannily like the ghost in the other room. Only this woman was clearly solid and alive.

What was going on here?

After a moment, Chris spoke up. "Can we help you?"

The woman cried out in surprise and turned in our direction. At the same time she reached for a light switch on the wall.

The lights came on.

Despite my effort not to, I cried out in horror. The right side of the woman's face was normal—beautiful even. But the left side was hideously scarred, as if something had pulled at it, tugging the flesh toward her neck. Her eye, her cheek, the side of her mouth all twisted down, and thick ridges of scar tissue marched across her cheek and forehead like mountains on one of those three-dimensional maps they have in museums.

"Who are you?" she hissed. "What are you doing here?"

Even as I was trying to find my voice, the woman was pulling her long hair over the side of her face, trying to mask the deformity. But the wet strands clung together, making bars down her face through which the scars still showed.

That was when I realized she was soaking wet. Glancing down, I saw a little puddle forming around her on the floor—water dripping from her clothes.

Was this the woman who had caused us to run off the road? It didn't seem likely there would have been anyone else walking around in this weather, but our previous experiences had taught us that when a situation starts getting this weird you can't take anything for granted. Still, she was the most likely candidate. And it had been so hard to see in the dark and the rain that we could easily have missed her scars.

I wondered if she was dangerous.

"Who are you?" she repeated.

"My name is Nina Tanleven," I stammered. "This is my friend, Chris Gurley. We had an accident up the road and couldn't get help or a phone, so we're staying here for the night."

The woman made a little gasp. She had a terribly pained expression on her face. Before she could say anything, we heard a squawk from the other room.

"Don't go! Don't go!" cried Commander Cody.

The woman closed her one good eye and sighed.

Making a guess, I asked, "Is he talking to someone in particular?"

"Not unless you believe in ghosts," replied the woman.

"We do," said Chris. "In fact, we're sort of known for that."

The woman gave us an odd look. I could see the idea taking form in her head. "Are you those two kids I read about in the paper? The ones who solved the mystery at the Grand Theater?" Her voice was strangely eager. Even so, I was starting to feel a little more comfortable with her.

I nodded.

She shook her head. "I can't believe you ended up *here.*"

"Why not?" asked Chris.

"Because I need you so much," she said, starting to cry again.

Chris elbowed my ribs. "Told you," she whispered.

Ignoring her gloating, I went to the table and said quietly, "Mind if we sit down?"

The woman shook her head.

I pulled out a chair and slipped into it. Tugging the blanket around my shoulders, I realized how odd Chris and I must have looked to her when she saw us standing there. I waited for the woman to calm down a little. Then I put my hand on her arm and whispered, "Why do you need us?"

"I have to tell my mother I'm sorry," she moaned.

"Was that your mother we saw in the living room?" asked Chris.

The woman sat up so straight that I thought her chair was going to fall over. *"You saw her?"* she hissed, her one good eye widening in astonishment.

I sighed, wishing Chris had waited a little bit longer before dropping that particular bombshell.

Chris nodded, adding, "She was crying, too."

Tears welled up in the woman's eyes again.

"Don't," I said, tightening my grip on her arm. "Don't cry. Just tell us what's going on. Maybe we really can help."

And what if we can't? asked a little voice in the back of my head. I tried my best to ignore it.

The woman took a deep breath. Looking down at her hands, she whispered, "Twenty years ago this very night I killed my mother."

I felt my stomach twist. Were we sitting at the table with a homicidal maniac who might turn on us at any moment? I glanced around, hoping there were no butcher knives in easy reach.

"How did you kill her?" asked Chris, who seemed to take this news more calmly than I did. Maybe that was because Chris's mother was still around, whereas I hadn't seen mine since the day she took off to "find her own life." Mothers were less of an issue for her.

The woman gave us a very sad smile. "I didn't shoot her or anything like that. But I might as well have. I was supposed to go to a Halloween party with my boyfriend, Bud Hendricks. My mother didn't want me to go. 'Dolores, that boy is no good!' she kept saying. 'He'll only bring you grief.'

"We had a screaming battle. Finally she forbid me to leave the house. When Bud showed up, she turned him away at the door."

Dolores sighed. "Just after eleven o'clock I snuck out. I had managed to call Bud, and he was planning to meet me a mile up the road, so Mother wouldn't know what I was up to. She found out anyway, of course; she was brilliant at that kind of thing. And she went out after me. Dad was working late at his office, and Mom's car was in the shop, so she went on foot. That's how worried she was about me."

Dolores shivered. "When Bud picked me up, I realized that he had been drinking—which was one of the things Mom objected to about him. We started back toward town. The storm that had been building up all day cut loose. Bud was driving too fast, not paying enough attention . . ."

Dolores started to cry again, but after a moment she got hold of herself. "My mother was walking toward us through the rain. I saw her first. I screamed and grabbed the steering wheel. We swerved, but not enough. We hit my mother, then went rolling into the ditch and smashed against a tree. That's when this happened," she said, pulling back the hair that covered her terrible scars.

Neither Chris nor I knew what to say. Finally I just touched her arm and whispered, "What happened next?"

"I was in a coma for about a month," Dolores whispered at last. "When I came out of it, my father told me that both Bud and my mother were dead. He looked half dead himself." She turned away from us. "Dad never did recover from it all—though he took good care of me while I was recuperating." She sighed. "Poor Dad. He couldn't tell me about my face, just couldn't bring himself to be the one to do it. One of the nurses had to hand me the mirror . . ."

She choked on the memory. I watched her, glad that her telling the story had given me a chance to really study her face, and at the same time embarrassed that I wanted to study it. I felt sick in my stomach from the way it looked. What would it be like to go through life that way?

Dolores ran her fingers over the scars. "I don't mind them too much now," she said, almost as if she had read my mind. "They feel like a fitting punishment. What I mind is what I did—that, and the fact that I was never able to tell my mother how sorry I was, never got to take back my last words to her."

"Your last words?" asked Chris.

Dolores closed her eyes. "When we had our fight, I screamed that I hated her." She put her fingers against her scarred cheek, and I could see that they were trembling. "'I hate you!' I screamed. 'I hate you! I hate you!' Then I ran upstairs and slammed the door to my room." She paused, swallowed hard, then whispered, "Those were the last words I ever said to her."

I shivered. It wasn't hard to see why Dolores wanted so much to say something to her mother. I know lots of kids who have told their parents they hated them, but none who had had the bad luck to have their parents die before they got to take the words back.

"Have you ever seen your mother's ghost?" asked Chris.

Dolores shook her head.

"Then why did you think she was still around?" I asked.

"The parrot sees her."

She looked defensive, as if she was daring me to contradict her.

"How do you know the bird sees her?" asked Chris.

Dolores looked down at her hands. "He talks to her. He was her bird, she'd had him from before I was born." She smiled. "He always used to greet her when she walked into the room. 'Hello, Sweetie!' he would say. 'Hello, Sweetie!'"

Her smile faded, and she looked down at her hands. "The bird didn't say a word for six weeks after Mother died. Then one night after I came home from the hospital I was sitting in the living room when he let out an incredible squawk and cried, 'Hello, Sweetie! Hello, Sweetie!'"

Dolores's good eye grew very large as she remembered the night. "'Mother?' I called. 'Mother, are you there?'"

"I knew she was. But she didn't answer."

Dolores sat back in her chair. "She's haunted this house ever since. She comes about once a month. I never see her, but the bird always knows when she's here, always tells her hello, always cries 'Don't go! Don't go!' when she leaves, just like he did when she was alive."

She closed her eyes. "She must be so angry. I have to tell her how sorry I am. Maybe then her spirit can rest. I go out every year on this night, hoping maybe I will meet her along the road. But I never do." She paused, then said, "I'm terribly sorry about your car. When I saw it tonight, for a moment I thought . . ."

She looked away, her shoulders trembling. "It's almost identical to the car Bud was driving that night. I thought . . . oh, I don't know what I thought! I was so shocked I must have lost my mind for a moment. After you swerved away from me, I fainted. When I came to, I was horrified. I went to see if you were all right, but you had already left. I'm so sorry."

Now *this* was a situation my father never anticipated when he chose to drive an antique car. I was trying to figure out how he was going to react to Dolores's story when I heard Chris say softly, "Do you want to try something?"

Dolores and I both spoke at the same time. "What?"

Chris looked a little nervous. "Before I tell you, you have to realize there's a lot about this ghost stuff that Nine and I still don't understand yet ourselves. It does seem like the more experiences we have, the easier it gets for us to see them. The problem is, we're not the ones who need to see your mother. You are. But I'm wondering if we go in the living room and sit together, me on one side of you, Nine on the other, and hold hands—well, maybe it would bring you into the link so that you could see her, too."

The idea made me a little nervous; we had never actually tried to summon a ghost. And I wasn't sure what this ghost was going to be like. Just because she had been weeping when we saw her didn't mean she wasn't still in a screaming rage about what had happened twenty years ago. What would we do if she showed up angry? It's not like we had an instruction book with a chapter titled "How to Deal with a Really Furious Ghost."

On the other hand, I couldn't think of anything else to do. If fate had brought us here to help Dolores, this made as much sense as anything.

Dolores seemed to have pretty much the same reaction. "I'd do anything to see her again," she whispered.

"Shall we try it?" asked Chris, looking at me.

I nodded. Without another word, the three of us stood, and walked into the living room.

"Jeremiah," squawked the parrot as we entered the room. "Go to Jeremiah."

"That's the second time tonight he's said that," I whispered. "Who's Jeremiah?"

"I don't have the slightest idea," said Dolores. "I never heard him say it at all until about four months after the accident. It was as if he learned it after Mother's death—though neither my father nor I taught it to him. For a while, I wondered if it was someone that Mother wanted me to contact. I even looked in her address book. But she didn't know any Jeremiah."

One more bit of weirdness. I was trying to figure out how they all fit together.

We sat on the couch, Dolores between Chris and me. I was on her left side, the side with the scar.

"Now what?" asked Dolores.

"I don't know," I said. "I guess you should try to call your mother."

Dolores closed her eyes. "Mother," she whispered. "Mother, can you hear me?"

Nothing.

"Maybe Nine and I should try," said Chris. "Mrs. Smiley, if you can hear us, come back, come—"

She was interrupted by Commander Cody. "Hello, Sweetie!" he squawked. "Hello, Sweetie!"

Dolores's hand flinched in mine.

For a moment, we saw nothing, and I wondered if the bird was really an indicator that the ghost was around. Then Mrs. Smiley shimmered into view, a still-pretty, middle-aged lady whose face was marked by infinite sorrow.

Dolores gasped.

Mrs. Smiley looked at her daughter and shook her head sadly. I felt a surge of relief: At least she wasn't mad.

"Why are you here?" I asked.

No answer. I wasn't surprised. In all the times Chris and I have met ghosts, not one of them has ever spoken to us.

"Mother," whispered Dolores, "I am so sorry. Can you ever forgive me?"

I wondered if this would break whatever tie held the ghost, free her to go on to the next world. But Mrs. Smiley didn't go. Instead, she leaned over to the parrot, as if whispering to him.

"Jeremiah!" it squawked. "Go to Jeremiah!"

The ghost looked at us pleadingly, as if begging us to understand.

That was when I got it. "Was your mother very religious?" I whispered.

Dolores nodded. "*Very*. It was something else we fought about."

"Don't move. I'll be right back!"

I slipped my hand out of hers, half afraid the ghost would vanish once I did. But she stood in place, a look of desperate hope on her face. I tiptoed up the stairs and into the room Mr. Smiley had assigned to Chris and me.

The family Bible that lay on the dresser was covered with dust. I blew it off, then started to flip through the pages. It took me a moment to find the book of Jeremiah, but when I did, I struck pay dirt. Pressed between the pages were two thin sheets of paper, almost like the stuff you use for airmail. They were so thin you would never have known there was anything in the book if you weren't looking for it.

Glancing at the pages where the letter had been waiting, I saw that two phrases had been underlined in the text. The first was in chapter 31, verse 22: "How long wilt thou go about, O thou backsliding daughter?"

Yow, I thought. *That sure puts a finger on what Mrs. Smiley was all wound up about.*

But the second phrase, which was part of verse 34, gave me hope. It said, "I will forgive their iniquity, and I will remember their sin no more."

I glanced at the letter. The handwriting was wobbly, as if the person who wrote it had been very weak, and it looked unfinished. But I knew Dolores had to see it.

I slipped back down the stairs. When the ghost saw me, saw what I was holding, she burst into tears.

I thrust the letter into Dolores's hand. "Here," I said. "Read this."

She glanced at it. Then, with a quavering voice, she spoke aloud the words her mother had written nearly twenty years earlier—the undelivered letter her spirit had stayed to make sure her daughter finally read.

My Darling Dolores,

As I write these words, we both lie in hospital beds, with little hope that either of us will ever leave them. If the Lord must take one of us, I pray it will be me. You have a whole life ahead of you. I already have too much behind me.

I will have one great sorrow in dying, dear one, which is that I will not be here to see you grow to womanhood. I have, too, one great fear—not of death, for I trust the Lord. My fear is of dying before we can make peace between us.

Oh, my sweet baby girl, how can I say what is in my heart? How can I say how much I love you? You will not know until you are a mother yourself. I would do anything, give anything, to protect you

from the sorrow and pain that have come to you. I
am so sorry, my beloved. <u>More</u> than sorry.

There is one thing you must know if I should die
before you wake. <u>I forgive you.</u> For whatever part
you feel you played in this tragedy, I forgive you. For
whatever you fear I am angry about, I forgive you.
For whatever sorrow you think you have caused me,
I forgive you. For whatever wrong you believe you
have done me, I forgive you—as I hope that God and
you will forgive me.

Terrible things happen between mothers and
daughters, my dear one, but there is a ferocious love
that binds us. With all the love I have, I release you
from guilt.

Do you remember when you were little and we
used to read <u>The Hunting of the Snark</u>? The Bellman
said, "What I tell you three times is true." You used
to repeat that whenever you wanted to convince me
of something. Now I am telling <u>you</u> three times: I
forgive you, I forgive you, I forgive you

That was as far as Mrs. Smiley had written. She must
have tucked the letter into the Bible, then died before
she could finish it. As her daughter read it aloud now,

Mrs. Smiley's ghost drifted toward us. Kneeling before her daughter, she gazed at her with the most radiant look of love I have ever seen.

Something twisted inside me as I wondered where my own mother had gone.

After a moment Mrs. Smiley reached her hand toward Dolores's face. She couldn't touch her, of course. That's the thing with ghosts—their forms are less than mist, and no matter how they try, they just can't touch you. So Dolores didn't realize her mother was there until I whispered, "Dolores, look up."

She raised her head and gasped. Tears streaming down her cheeks, flowing through the valleys of her scars, she whispered, "Oh Mother, I miss you, I miss you, I miss you."

Mrs. Smiley nodded in understanding. Yet she seemed sad as well. She looked up, and I saw an expression of great longing on her pale, glowing face.

"You have to let go of her, Dolores," I whispered. "She didn't stay all these years because she was angry. She stayed because you needed to know she loved you, needed to know she forgave you. *She stayed because you hadn't let go of her.*"

"Nine's right," said Chris. "You have to let her move on now."

I could see Dolores swallow. "I love you, Mother," she whispered. "I miss you. And . . . I release you."

She said it three times.

I thought it was over. But from the darkness, from a place beyond understanding, another visitor arrived.

It was a young man, pale and transparent, yet quite handsome.

"Bud!" whispered Dolores.

The new ghost smiled at Dolores sadly. Then he floated toward us, bent, and pressed his lips against her scarred cheek. He could not really touch it, of course. But Dolores knew what he was telling her. Raising her trembling fingers to her face, she watched as Bud took Mrs. Smiley's hand and began to lead her away from us— out of this world with its sorrows and rages and tragedies, on to a place of perfect forgiveness.

Suddenly Mrs. Smiley stopped. Turning back to us, she blew her daughter one last kiss. Then she smiled again, turned, and vanished slowly into the darkness.

In the Frog King's Court

DENNIS JUGGARUM was squatting at the edge of Bingdorf's Swamp the first time he spotted the five-legged frog. The sight made him recoil in fear and disgust. Even so, he decided to catch the thing—partly because he was fascinated by it, and partly because he wanted to show it to his biology teacher, Mr. Crick. They had discussed mutations in class just a week or two earlier; maybe he could get extra credit for bringing this one in. Given his grades on the last two tests, that would be a good thing!

To his surprise, the frog's lopsided condition did nothing to slow it down. Extra leg flapping uselessly at its side, the creature easily leaped away before he could lay hands on it.

"Drat!" muttered Dennis. He cursed mostly out of habit, since he was actually relieved not to touch the thing. Part of him—not his brain, but something deep in his gut—feared that whatever caused the weird mutation might be contagious.

That fear didn't stop Dennis from returning to the swamp the next afternoon. But then, he had done that nearly every day for the last six years. For some reason he felt at home there—certainly more at home than he ever did in school, where some oaf was always ready to tease him about his looks, or, more specifically, about his bulging eyes.

He had long ago given up complaining to his mother about the teasing. "Oh, Dennis, what nonsense!" she would scoff. "You're a *very* handsome boy." Which, oddly enough, he knew to be almost true. All he needed to be as handsome as a prince was eyeball-reduction surgery.

In the swamp he could forget about his looks, about school, about teasing, about everything that bugged him in his daily life. The only thing he couldn't ignore was the smokestacks of the Bingdorf chemical factory on the far side of the swamp—the only blot on an otherwise beautifully untamed view. Even though everyone in town was sure the plant was dumping its toxic wastes here, no one had been able to prove it. According to his mother, most people didn't want it proved, preferring jobs to clean water. And since old man Bingdorf owned not only the factory but also the swamp, he was able to get away with it.

Dennis forced his eyes away from the distant silhouette of the hated factory. Today he had come to the swamp for a more specific purpose than simply losing himself in the buzz and pulse of life that surrounded him whenever he was here. Having bombed his third bio test in a row, he was determined to catch the mutant frog. The need for extra credit had grown to emergency proportions!

Squatting a few feet from the murky water, holding himself motionless, Dennis cast his glance in all directions. He gasped. Barely an arm's length to his right squatted the five-legged frog—and next to it a frog with eyes on its shoulders! The eyes blinked, causing Dennis to cry out and stumble backward. At the sound of his voice the frogs leaped away, disappearing with a *plunk* under a mat of algae.

Dennis wasn't sure whether he was disappointed— or relieved.

When he told his mother about the mutated frogs that night she frowned and said, "I've been reading about that problem in other places, Den. They're pretty sure it's caused by chemical pollution. Around here, that would mean the Bingdorf factory, of course. Not that old man Bingdorf would care. He'd sell his own children if he thought he could get a decent price for the chemicals they were made of. But you'd better stay out of the swamp, Dennis. I don't want three-legged grandchildren!"

Though Dennis rarely rebelled against a parental order, he couldn't resist the weirdness of what he had seen—or the chance for that extra credit in bio. So the next afternoon found him back in the swamp, frog hunting again. At least, that was the reason he gave himself. The truth was, he would have gone even without the lure of the mutants. The swamp was just too important to his peace of mind for him to abandon it so easily.

His defiance of his mother's orders paid off when he spotted the five-legged frog again. This time it was sitting alone. Gathering his courage, Dennis crept forward, hands cupped and ready. But just as he was about to lunge for it, the frog leaped away.

Dennis splashed into the swamp after it.

Aside from the fact that it would make his mother angry, going into the water didn't seem dangerous. He had waded into the swamp plenty of times before and knew it was less than two feet deep here.

At least, it had never been more than two feet deep in the past. To his shock, Dennis now found himself up to his thighs in water.

Even worse, his feet were stuck in the muddy bottom. No, worse than stuck. He was sinking!

Quicksand! was his first, terrified thought. *I've stumbled into quicksand!*

Then something else happened, something so appallingly weird that it drove the thought of quicksand from his mind. He saw a virtual army of deformed frogs swimming toward him, some with missing legs, others with five, six, or even seven legs; some were absurdly small, others horrifyingly large; some had split faces or extra eyes, or were weirdly colored. Dennis cried out in horror as the little monstrosities clambered onto his shoulders, then his head. The clammy flesh of their bellies pressing against the skin of his face drove him mad with fear. They seemed to be weighing him down, pushing him into the soft, sucking bottom of the swamp.

Dennis's screams were cut off as his head went under the surface. The muck—well past his thighs now, nearly to his waist—was holding him, clutching him. Wild with terror, he flailed his arms, churning the water like a propeller.

It did no good.

He opened his eyes. Through the dimly lit water, green and murky, he saw that the swarm of frogs was growing thicker, more dense. Hundreds—no, *thousands*— of frogs were swimming closer, pushing him deeper into the swamp.

Choking on his fear, Dennis continued his descent into the muddy bottom. The ooze, more frightening than mere water, crept up his neck. When he felt it on his chin he opened his mouth to scream again. A tiny frog slipped inside. Revolted, he spit it out and clamped his lips shut.

The muck crept past his mouth, beyond his nose.

Finally it closed above his head.

When Dennis woke he was lying facedown on a patch of damp grass. Insects buzzed around him. Under their music he heard the song of frogs—the trill of spring peepers, the tenor tones of the small frogs he used to catch in the swamp, the deep baritone of the great bulls. He rolled over, then yelped in fear.

Instead of the distant blue sky, Dennis saw above him a vast expanse of muddy brown, seemingly no more than a few hundred feet away. Directly overhead the brown was replaced by a translucent green circle. The dim light filtering through the circle made him wonder if it was the bottom of the swamp.

He took a deep breath, testing the air. It was damp but pleasant. Tree-sized mushrooms grew all around him. Dennis pushed himself to his feet, delighted at finding himself still alive. "Unless this is where you go after you die," he muttered uneasily.

"Trust me, you're quite fine," said a deep, throaty voice.

Dennis spun in the direction of the voice. Sitting several feet away was a frog the size of a golden retriever. Its bulging eyes were the size of Ping-Pong balls.

"Who are *you*?" cried Dennis.

"Your guide. The king wants to see you. Follow me."

Without waiting for Dennis to respond, it began leaping toward the mushroom forest.

"Sure," said Dennis. "Follow you. Why not? Since I'm either dead or dreaming, I might as well."

The frog, clearly not listening, continued leaping into the forest. Not wanting to be left behind, Dennis scrambled to catch up.

The path they followed curved snakelike through the mushrooms. At some point the oppressively low "sky" was replaced by a decently distant one, which would have made Dennis feel better if not for the fact that it was bright green.

The sun—or whatever they called the glowing ball that lit the sky here—was green, too, the light green of early spring grass.

Dennis wanted to question his guide. But though the huge frog never got out of sight, it always managed to stay far enough ahead that Dennis wasn't able to talk to it.

Eventually the mushroom forest gave way to a vast swamp.

"Awesome," whispered Dennis, staring at ferns that grew as tall as trees and lily pads the size of the dining room carpet. A jewel-eyed dragonfly buzzed past, its wings as long as Dennis's arms.

Still following his guide, Dennis hopped along strips of squishy land and crossed mucky areas on chains of grassy hummocks. Thick ooze bubbled and popped on all sides. Finally they came to a pair of towering willows that formed a natural archway.

"This is as far as I go," said his guide. "Beyond these trees lies the Court of King Urpthur, Lord of All Frogs. Be courteous and respectful when you greet him."

"But—"

The frog held up its front feet. "The king will tell you all you need to know. Go in."

Stepping between the willows, Dennis caught his breath in wonder. Before him stretched a courtroom of elegant beauty. Though it had no walls, its boundaries were clearly marked by stems of mushroom and fern. Growing far straighter here than anywhere else he had seen them, they formed a series of alternating green and beige pillars. The caps of the mushrooms spread like giant umbrellas, while the fern fronds curled high to create a lacy green roof.

In the center of the court shimmered a long pond filled with water lilies, their soup-bowl-sized blossoms displaying a thousand shades of pink, yellow, and white. Along the sides of the pond, standing on their hind legs and chatting casually, were dozens of frogs, most taller than Dennis. Many wore hats and capes and had swords buckled about their waists.

At the far side of the pond, on an ornate throne carved directly into the giant trunk of a living willow, sat King Urpthur. His golden crown was studded with emeralds. A scarlet cape hung from his shoulders. The green fingers of his right hand curled around a golden scepter. Next to the throne was a gong, suspended from a willow frame.

The court fell silent when Dennis entered. All eyes—
and big, goggling eyes they were—turned to him.

"Come forward," croaked the king.

Dennis did as he was asked. But when he reached the
edge of the pond he stopped, uncertain. Was he supposed
to wade through it or pick his way around it? Looking
more carefully, he was relieved to spot a faint path on the
grassy bank. Following it around the pond to a spot directly in front of the king, he paused, uncertain of what
to do next. Finally remembering his guide's warning to
be "courteous and respectful," he made an awkward
bow.

King Urpthur smiled, which pretty much split his
face in half. "Greetings, Dennis, and welcome to my
court! Please accept my apologies for the frightening way
we brought you here. It is difficult to transport a human
to Froglandia, and getting more difficult as the years go
by. We only brought you now because of the extreme
danger in which we find ourselves."

"The mutations!" guessed Dennis out loud.

Immediately he wondered if he should have spoken
without being asked. But the king merely nodded, his
face grave and frightened. "The mutations," he repeated
softly.

"I understand they would upset you. But what do they have to do with me?"

"You are one of our links to the human world."

"I beg your pardon?"

"Granted."

Dennis blushed. "I mean, I don't understand."

"Oh. Oh, I see!" The king began to laugh, a deep, rich *chug-a-rumming*. The court joined in, until the result was almost deafening, a percussion concert of croaking.

"As I was saying," said the king, after he recovered from his mirth, "you are part of the frog family." Seeing the doubt on Dennis's face, he continued, "Your nineteenth great-grandfather on your mother's side was what is sometimes called a frog prince. There is often a misunderstanding about this in the old tales. In this case, the princess who kissed the frog was *not* turning an enchanted human back into his own form. She was turning one of my own ancestors (Great-Uncle Hopgo, to be precise—we royal frogs have quite long lives) into a human! Personally, I think it was silly of Unc to give up Froglandia, and his life span, for a mere human. But love does that to frogs.

"Anyway, the point is that you, Dennis, have a small but still significant component of frog blood within you, waiting to assert itself. This explains, by the way, why you have been attracted to swamps all your life."

"But—"

"Oh, don't try to deny it. We've watched you gaze longingly into our murky waters. We've listened to your sighs. Search your heart, Dennis Juggarum. Isn't it true that when you stand at the edge of the swamp something in your blood cries out, 'Home. That's *home!*'"

Dennis stared at the king in astonishment. Speaking very slowly, he said, "You're telling me that I'm part frog?"

"Yes. A distant relative, in fact."

Dennis gulped and hoped his eyes weren't bulging too much.

"Of course, you're not the only cousin-several-times-removed we have wandering around the human world," continued the king. "But you are the only one who happened to be close to a swamp at the moment, which meant you were the one we turned to for help. After all, we can't just go hopping into the city and haul people off the streets." He chuckled at the thought, the sound reverberating in his enormous throat.

"What is it, exactly, that you want me to do?" asked Dennis uneasily.

The king's tongue flicked out and snagged a passing

insect the size of a small bird. He swallowed, then said, "As you have seen, my subjects are suffering disastrous effects from the chemicals being leaked into the water. Frogdom has many levels, of course, and at the moment it is only the smallest of my people who are suffering— the ones tied most closely to your world. But that which happens to the least of my subjects is of concern to me. Am I not their king? What I want, Dennis, is for you to go to the man causing the pollution and make him stop!"

"He won't listen to me. I'm just a kid."

"He'll listen if you go to him as a giant talking frog."

Cold fear prickled along Dennis's neck. When he finally managed to speak past his confusion, the words came as a whispered "You want me to become a frog?"

"Exactly!" cried the king, leaping to his feet. "I want you to arise as the righteous avenger of all frogdom and terrify these despoilers of our waters. Hop into their hearts as a symbol of the wrath of nature—nature aroused and angry—nature that will rend them from limb to limb if they persist in their evil ways. I want you, Dennis, to become a crusading frog of doom!"

"You want me to become a frog," whispered Dennis again.

"Oh, not permanently," said the king, airily waving a long green hand. "You're not built for it, long term.

But just as tadpoles transform themselves into frogs, you have the bloodlines to do the same thing. You just need a little . . . prodding."

"What kind of prodding?" asked Dennis out loud. In his mind he was saying, *Don't panic. It's only a dream!*

Reaching out with his scepter, the king struck the gong that hung next to his throne. Its clang was like the croak of a metallic frog.

"Yeah, yeah, yeah," grumbled a hoarse voice, the words seeming to come from the ground itself. "I'll be there in a minute."

A sudden hiss of steam beside the throne made Dennis step back. The ground bubbled, which was an alarming sight, and the steam gathered into a swirling cloud that turned green then vanished. In its place stood a stoop-shouldered old frog with wire-rimmed glasses perched on his nose. He wore a dark green robe covered with stars and moons. Cupped between his green fingers was a wooden goblet with lilies carved around its stem. Steam flowed over the edge of the goblet, falling to the ground like mist. There it curled around the old frog's feet until he appeared to be standing in a small cloud. He grinned at Dennis. "Nice entrance, huh, kid?"

"Amazing! Um, who are you?"

"Don't tell me you never heard of Murklin the Mudgician. Oh, forget it. I don't wanna know. Here, drink this."

He extended the steaming goblet to Dennis.

"What will happen if I do?"

"It will release your inner frog," said King Urpthur happily, "and make the destiny written in your blood clear for all to see!"

Dennis continued to stare at the goblet, which burped and blurped with little pops of muddy liquid. "What if I don't want to release my inner frog?"

An angry murmur rose behind him. "Traitor," he heard low voices croak. "Ingrate!"

The king raised a hand to silence the court. "We will not force you to do this. But if you refuse, you will forever bear the knowledge that you abandoned both kin and king in their hour of need. You will know you let fear, not courage, rule your heart. You will forever remember yourself as one not willing to shed your skin for a greater cause."

"But I don't *want* to be a frog!"

"Part of you already is. A small part, granted. But part of you, nevertheless. Besides, it's not permanent. You'll only be a frog sometimes."

"When?"

"The night before and the night after the full moon

are what we call frog moons. On those sacred nights you can rise in frogly glory to confront the villains who are poisoning my subjects. Oh, Dennis, Dennis—think of it! To how many men is it given to find the secrets hidden in their blood, to wear two shapes, to live two lives? To how many men is it given to speak truth to power, to be a voice for their people? How many, how many, are allowed to croak for the good of others?"

Inspired by the king's words, Dennis reached for the goblet. Its warmth felt good between his hands. He gazed into it.

The bubbling, popping brew looked like a miniature swamp.

This is my destiny, he told himself, lifting the cup to his lips. *Besides, it's only a dream, so what difference does it make?*

The brew smelled of the swamp, of wildness, of magic. The first swallow was difficult. Then the potion took hold of him. Surrendering to it, Dennis drained the cup to the last drop.

The assembled frogs burst into ribbiting cheers as the world swirled green around him.

When Dennis woke he was lying at the edge of the swamp, the hot sun beating down on his face, his clothes clean and dry.

Beside him sat the five-legged frog. Dennis reached for it, but it leaped away, disappearing into the swamp with a small splash.

He sighed and pushed himself to his feet, muttering, "What a weird dream. I must be coming down with something."

"Dennis, where have you been?" cried his mother when he came through the door. "Dinner was ready half an hour ago!"

"I was out visiting some . . . friends." Then, on a whim, he asked, "Mom, did we ever have any royalty in our family?"

His mother smiled. "Well, according to Gramma Wetzel, your nineteenth great-grandfather on my side was a genuine prince."

His horrified reaction must have shown on his face, for she said quickly, "What's wrong, Dennis?"

"Nothing! I just don't feel very well."

It *was* nothing. It had to be nothing.

He clung to that thought all night.

Even so, when he went to his room after supper, he opened his window and pushed up the screen—just in case he needed to get out later on.

Eventually Dennis fell into a fitful sleep, marked by

dreams that were strange and soggy. When he awoke, the moon was shining through his window. As he remembered from the night before, it was round and nearly full—nearly, but not quite.

A frog moon.

Suddenly Murklin's potion began its strange work. Dennis's eyes began to bulge more than ever. He grabbed for his ears, but they were shrinking—shrinking—*gone!* Sliding his hands upward, he felt his hair disappearing into his clammy skin. Looking down, he saw his legs grow longer, stronger, and greener.

An instant later his terror was replaced by a rending pain that seared him from head to toe.

And then it was over, the transformation complete.

Staggering to his feet, Dennis found that despite having become a frog he was still his regular height, maybe even a bit taller. Clearly he was the kind of frog he had seen at the king's court. He held his hands before him, marveling at his long, green fingers and the webbing that stretched between them.

A cool night breeze lifted the curtains, carrying with it the odor of the swamp. Dennis found the smell irresistible. He scrambled over the sill and onto the lawn, where he dropped to jumping position.

The cool, dew-laden grass felt sweet against his flat

white belly. He blinked twice, took another deep breath of the moist air. Then, without really thinking about it, he unleashed the power of his mighty legs.

The force of his leap sent him hurtling into the air.

Too high! he thought, as he soared across the yard, his heart hammering in terror. *I'm going too high!*

Yet when he landed and realized he had survived the leap, he felt a surge of joy. *It's almost like flying!*

Flexing his legs again, Dennis bounded gleefully around the lawn, leaping higher and higher.

A chorus of tiny peeps brought him to a halt.

He turned. The field behind the house looked as if it was starting to percolate. Then he saw the cause. Leaping toward him were his . . . well, his cousins: thousands of frogs, tiny ones in the lead, larger ones—though not so large as him, of course—bringing up the rear.

The frog moon floated above them like an enormous silver coin.

His cousins surrounded him, an avenging army of frogdom. The littlest ones crept forward to stare up at him, their goggling eyes awash with admiration.

Dennis felt a sense of purpose surge through him. Taking a deep breath, he puffed out his throat and emitted a sound that astonished even him, a deep bass note, a trumpet call of warning that reverberated through the night—the sound of a mighty amphibian who had had enough.

Fire in his froggy eyes, Dennis turned to lead his leaping army toward old man Bingdorf's estate.

Someone had to stop that man's polluting ways.

Someone had to protect the water.

Someone had to say, "This is enough. You cannot do this any longer!"

And he, Dennis Juggarum, was just the frog to do it.

The Thing in Auntie Alma's Pond

WATER.

Margaret hated water.

So why was she standing at the edge of Auntie Alma's pond, staring at the black water as if she could see more than a few inches past the murky surface?

As if she were looking for something.

A dragonfly darted past, its flashing emerald wings startling Margaret out of her thoughts. She raised her eyes to gaze again at the little rowboat that floated in the pond. It seemed strange to see it caught in the middle like that, not free to drift to one side or the other.

Why is it anchored there, anyway? she wondered uneasily. She shrugged. Probably one of her cousins had done it. They were always playing pranks.

The thought of her cousins made her sigh. It would be nice if a few of them were around now. Auntie Alma's place was just too quiet without them. Sure, their rowdiness annoyed her sometimes. Even so, they would liven things up a bit. She sighed again. If only that rowboat was back on the shore, where she could get at it.

Turning, she started back toward the house. It would be a long time before she forgave her parents for leaving her here like this. Their separation had been bad enough. Now, to "work on getting back together," they had shoved her off on Auntie Alma . . . left her here to rot for the summer while they tried to "find themselves." Why didn't they try to find *her*, instead? She had been feeling lost for some time now, and being exiled from her home and friends like this was no help.

Margaret kicked savagely at a silver dandelion, setting its seeds free to float away on the breeze. If her parents *did* have to send her away for the summer, couldn't they have found someplace besides Auntie Alma's? Sure, it was out in the country, and the fresh air was probably good for her. But there was no one around to hang out with, no one to even talk to except Auntie Alma, who wasn't her real aunt anyway, for heaven's sake, just an old friend of the family.

A really old friend, if you wanted to get right down to it, thought Margaret unkindly. Indeed, white-haired Alma Jefferson was a truly ancient collection of crotchets and wrinkles. She had a huge, hairy mole on her chin that Margaret found simultaneously fascinating and repugnant. Her hearing was bad, her eyes were weak, and she put her teeth in a glass on the kitchen shelf every night. Margaret especially hated that. Something about the sight of those dead things soaking in their cold water always made her shiver.

Stop it, she told herself as she went through the back door of the house. *You're being cruel.*

In fact, pausing to think about it made Margaret remember how much she had loved Auntie Alma when she, Margaret, was younger—how when she was frightened she would throw her arms around the old woman's waist and whisper, "I'm always safe with you."

That memory made it all the more painful when Margaret entered the kitchen and saw the slight look of disappointment that flickered across Auntie Alma's face. Though the expression vanished almost instantly, it stabbed Margaret to the heart. *I guess she doesn't want me around, either. Probably she was hoping I'd drown while I was out at the pond.*

Margaret shuddered at the thought. She had been afraid of Auntie Alma's pond for as long as she could remember—which wouldn't have been quite so bad if everyone else in the family hadn't seemed to think it was the most wonderful place in the world.

How they had teased her for not wanting to enter its cool, dark waters. "For heaven's sake, Margaret, come in and cool off," her mother would exclaim on those hot summer afternoons when they came here to escape the city. "You like the pool in town. What's wrong with this?"

But Margaret could never explain her fear of the pond, the sense of nameless dread that seized her whenever she stood on its grassy bank and imagined stepping down into the black water.

The feeling that something was *waiting* for her there.

That was why she had always preferred the boat. It held her safely above the pond, its wooden floor a comforting barrier between herself and the terrifying water.

Still, those fears had been only a small part of her life back in what she now thought of as the good old days—the time when Mom and Dad had been happy together, not acting as if being married was some miserable job they had been forced into against their will. She sighed. Why did grown-ups have to make such a big deal out of everything, anyway?

She wished her friend Annie could have come here

with her. Or better yet, that she could have stayed at Annie's house, where she always felt welcome and wanted.

Auntie Alma made supper and set it on the table. "A summer supper," she said cheerfully, as she always did when she put out this kind of meal. It consisted of nothing but fresh things from her garden: thick sliced tomatoes, red as blood, each bite packed with more flavor than a dozen of the pale, hard things Margaret's mother bought at the grocery store in the winter; yellow squash, glistening with melted butter, seeds nearly clear from the steaming; and baby carrots, torn early from the ground.

The only thing not from the garden was dessert—Auntie Alma's special molasses cookies. Though Margaret had loved these when she was little, tonight she couldn't bring herself to touch them.

"Goodness, pumpkin," clucked the old woman. "You haven't eaten a thing."

Margaret stared at the soft face, which quivered with concern. Unable to contain herself anymore, she shouted, "I want to go home!"

The look of sorrow that welled up in Auntie Alma's eyes was too much to bear. Margaret bolted from the table and fled to her room.

————

For the next hour she lay on her bed, staring at the ceiling. She was being horrible, and she knew it. Auntie Alma hadn't done anything wrong, had only been worried about her. But Margaret couldn't help herself. Nothing seemed right, and the knot of fear that had tied itself inside her gut left no room for food—not even Auntie Alma's cooking, which was, she had to admit, delicious.

But not now.

Not now.

At last Margaret slept—slept, but did not really rest, for in her dreams a familiar voice was calling to her, urging her to come into the darkness.

She woke with a gasp.

To her horror, the voice was still calling—not out loud, but inside her somehow, whispering in soft, oddly familiar tones, *Margaret, please come to me! Please, I need you to come to me!*

She clung to her bed, riveted by terror. Though she couldn't say what was calling, she knew all too well where the voice was coming from.

The pond.

As she had always known would happen one day, something in those murky waters was after her—desperately, urgently summoning her to come to it.

"I won't go," she whispered, tightening herself against the bed as if she could actually press herself into the mattress, merge with it so that nothing could pull her away. "I *won't* go!"

The voice called and pleaded, until finally Margaret shouted out in terror. That brought Auntie Alma bustling in to sit beside the bed and try to comfort her. The old woman's face was sad, and her wise old eyes seemed to hold some awful secret. But her voice was soothing and, even better, her muttered reassurances about bad dreams managed to drown out the voice that still called so longingly, so seductively, from the pond.

Finally Margaret fell asleep again.

When she woke, she noticed water on the floor.

From the dank smell, she knew it had come from the pond.

Late the next morning, somewhat to her astonishment, Margaret found herself standing once more at the edge of Auntie Alma's pond. A surge of panic rippled through her. How had she gotten here? She certainly didn't remember the walk! She swallowed nervously. Was whatever waited beneath the water so strong it could draw her here against her will? How much longer could she go on resisting?

She forced herself to back away from the water. After three steps, she turned and ran up the ridge that separated the pond from Auntie Alma's house.

Halfway to the crest she stopped and looked back.

The boat still floated in the center of the pond. The black water surrounding it was smooth and mirrorlike. The hot air held no hint of a breeze, as if the world itself were holding its breath.

Margaret looked past the boat to the far side of the pond, where a row of willows stood so close to the water it looked as if they were about to go wading. Their long, drooping branches overhung the pond, shading it for much of the day. Fallen leaves, narrow and shaped like the tips of spears, dotted the surface of the water, floating aimlessly.

Beyond the willows the land sloped up to a forested area, dark and mysterious yet somehow as inviting as the pond was terrifying.

Standing here now, Margaret remembered a summer day years earlier when she had been playing at the edge of the water. She had been three, maybe four, years old, and she was sitting happily on the grassy bank. Suddenly her uncle Ted had reared up from the pond, murky water streaming from his long hair, green weeds dangling from his grasping fingers. "I'm going to get you, Margaret!" he growled, stalking forward. "I'm going to get you!"

She had shrieked and run for her mother, which caused the assembled grown-ups—all the aunts and uncles and cousins—to laugh uproariously. Only Auntie Alma had disapproved, and Margaret still remembered with satisfaction the way the old woman had bawled out Uncle Ted.

Since then Margaret had often watched grown-ups play with children; she was still amazed at the way adults seemed to think it was fun to frighten little kids. Yet frequently the kids laughed. Did they really find the scares funny, or were they just trying to hide their fear? Was it possible they actually liked being frightened? If so, why didn't she? Was she really that different from all the others?

Probably, Margaret thought bitterly. *I've always been different. I should be used to it by now.*

With a start, she realized that Auntie Alma was standing beside her. How had the old woman walked up without her noticing?

"Are you all right, dear?"

Margaret didn't answer right away. She wasn't all right, not really. But she didn't think there was anything Auntie Alma could do to change that—except send her home, of course. Which didn't seem likely.

"I'm afraid," whispered Margaret at last, startling herself by letting the words escape.

Auntie Alma nodded. "It's hard when things change. Gets a person all stirred up inside."

Margaret relaxed a little. Maybe Auntie Alma understood better than she thought. She waited a moment, then said cautiously, "I'm afraid of the pond."

Auntie Alma didn't answer right away. When she did, her voice was soft and sounded far away. "No need to be afraid of it anymore. Not now."

"What does that mean?"

The old woman laughed. "If I told you everything you wanted to know, it wouldn't leave anything for you to find out on your own."

"Good thing you're not a teacher."

"Oh, the very best teachers never tell you everything, my dear. The *best* teachers know that you have to figure some things out for yourself." She smiled. "After all, what's life without a little mystery?"

"Safe," grumbled Margaret. But she said it so softly that Auntie Alma didn't seem to hear.

When Margaret climbed into bed that night, rain was pattering lightly against the window. She listened to it for a long time, staring into the darkness and unable to sleep.

Slowly, and to her great horror, she began to hear words in the rain—the same words she had heard the night before, now clearer and stronger than ever. Over and over they whispered, "Come to me, Margaret. Oh *please* come to me."

"Leave me alone!" she shouted at last.

At least, she thought she had shouted it. But since Auntie Alma didn't come in to find out what was wrong, maybe she hadn't shouted after all. She shuddered. Had the thing, whatever it was, stolen her voice?

She tried again. *"Leave me alone!"*

That sounded real enough. Why didn't Auntie Alma come?

She tried the direct approach. "Auntie Alma! Auntie Alma, I need you!"

No answer. No sound except the falling water and the voice that came from within it, calling her name, calling her to the pond.

A cold dread grew inside her. Where was Auntie Alma? Why didn't she come?

Part of her longed to fling aside the covers and go in search of the old woman, while another part of her shrank in terror from the thought of leaving the bed.

She lay, trembling, until the voice finally left her alone.

It was hours before she slept.

In the morning, there were puddles of pond water on her floor again. The sight terrified Margaret so thoroughly she couldn't bring herself to get out of bed until Auntie Alma came to her door to see if she was all right.

"Why didn't you come when I called last night?" asked Margaret angrily.

The round old face wrinkled in dismay. "I'm sorry, child. I must have gone out."

"Out in the rain?"

"I like the rain. And the nighttime. They're beautiful, if you pay attention."

"But I was frightened!"

"I'm sorry, pumpkin. But there isn't any reason to be frightened. No reason at all."

Margaret wished that not being afraid was as easy as Auntie Alma made it sound.

That afternoon she went for a walk in the opposite direction from the pond, following a faint trail that wound through the meadow on the north side of the house. She grew uneasy as she moved between the walls of high grass. At first she was uncertain why. Then she remembered what lay at the end of the path: the small family cemetery where the last three generations of Jeffersons had been buried. She thought about turning back, then decided against it. The cemetery wasn't really scary. In fact, it was a nice place to sit and think. She had gone there several times with her cousin Peter last summer, and they had talked about everything they wanted to do when they grew up.

She reached it now, walking under a thick branch of a low-growing apple tree that nearly blocked the path. The spot was much as she remembered it: a small clearing—about the same size as the pond, actually—hedged all around with brush and brambles that were starting to creep their way into the cemetery itself.

Fifteen or twenty white stones, some cracked, others severely tilted, marked the haphazardly arranged graves. Wild roses twined over many of the stones, and a variety of flowers grew on and around the low mounds that rose over the final resting places of Auntie Alma's relatives. Alma had told Margaret that she would probably be the last one to be buried here. She had no children of her own, and none of her nieces and nephews seemed to want a spot here. Margaret thought that was a little sad.

She sat beneath the apple tree and listened to the birds. The warm sun felt good on her skin. After a while she got up and began to read the gravestones, calculating the ages of various Jeffersons when they had died. The set

that got to her, and always had, was a group of four—
mother, father, and two children. What brought a lump
to Margaret's throat each time she read the stones was
that the husband and children had all died within a year
of each other, leaving the mother to live on alone for another fifty years. Her messages on the tombstones—
carved into each were the words I WILL LOVE YOU FOR
ALL OF MY LIFE followed by MOTHER, MOTHER, and then
WIFE—always struck Margaret as both beautiful and infinitely sad.

At the south side of the little clearing she noticed a
grave that she didn't remember. The stone was not
weathered, and the grave itself was not overgrown the
way the others were.

The skin at the back of Margaret's neck prickled as if
she had caterpillars crawling across it. A horrified feeling
growing in her chest, she walked to the grave and knelt
to read the stone.

Alma Jefferson, Beloved Friend

And the date—this past April.

With a cry of horror, Margaret turned and ran from
the cemetery. She raced along the path, the grass whipping at her legs. Halfway to the house she suddenly

stopped. How could she go back there, back to the old woman who was dead? She had to call her parents, tell them to come and get her.

Only she didn't know where they were.

Margaret stopped.

How could they have left her here to begin with?

The world seemed to swirl around her. Finally fear overwhelmed her, and she blacked out.

When Margaret woke it was to the music of crickets singing in the grass. The moon was riding low at the edge of the sky, pale and insubstantial, yet somehow comforting nonetheless. She remembered her teacher explaining that Shakespeare had had Juliet call the moon "inconstant" because it changed every night, moving through each month from nothing to fullness and back to nothing again. That might be, but at least it always came back. That was constant enough for Margaret right now. Its pale presence was like an old friend.

Like Auntie Alma.

Margaret stood still for a moment, then made up her mind. Auntie Alma had taken good care of her, hadn't tried to hurt her, would never try to hurt her. There was nothing in the house to be afraid of. Maybe the old woman even needed her help.

Telling herself this, ignoring the deeper, stranger questions that fought for her attention, Margaret made her way back to the house.

It was empty.

Somehow she had known it would be. Even so, a chill crept over her. Where was Auntie Alma? Or, to be more specific: Where had her ghost gone? Margaret had read enough ghost stories to have some idea of how this might work. She feared that the discovery of the tombstone had driven the ghost away.

Leaving her here alone.

Why was she here alone?

It grew darker. Margaret thought about getting something to eat, but her stomach was too tight for that.

And then the calling began again.

Margaret. Mar-gar-et. Come to me. Please, please come to me.

Was it Auntie Alma calling?

No. It wasn't her voice.

But if not her, then who?

Or what?

The house was too dark and lonely to protect her. The call had grown too strong to resist. Margaret began to weep—not great sobs, just a slow, gentle flow of tears down her cheeks. Against her will, she drifted through the door. With no light save that of the pale moon, she walked through the backyard, past the grape arbor, along the overgrown path, over the ridge to the pond.

Fireflies drifted above the dew-soaked grass, their brief, pale lights flashing on and off. But the crickets had fallen silent, as if waiting for something. No breeze stirred the surface of the water. The moon's reflection in the pond seemed that of a ghost moon floating, waiting.

And on the other side of the water, standing among the willows, was Auntie Alma.

Pale, translucent Auntie Alma, her color the same as that of the moon in the water, who held out her hands longingly to Margaret, imploring the child to come to her.

"I can't!" wailed Margaret. "I can't! I can't!"

But inside her mind the voice—not Auntie Alma's, the other voice—was whispering urgently, *Margaret, please! Come to me. It's time to stop pretending.*

Unable to resist, she walked to the edge of the water, to the same place she had found herself standing again and again for the last few days. The horror was growing inside her, filling her so full it seemed as if she must burst with it.

"Margaret!" called Auntie Alma from across the pond. "Margaret, dear, the only way out is in."

Margaret stood trembling in the darkness.

The only way out is in.

What was that supposed to mean? Actually, part of her knew exactly what it meant. Even so, she wanted to ask. But somehow she also knew that Auntie Alma couldn't tell her and had bent the rules to say even as much as she had.

She turned and ran, then stopped at the top of the rise and looked back. The pond lay black and still, the moon's reflection like a single enormous eye in its center.

The translucent woman still stood on the far side, waiting with open arms.

And from the water's depths came a call that she could no longer resist.

Slowly, Margaret walked down the hill, back to the edge of the water.

"The only way out is in," whispered Auntie Alma, her words clear and distinct across the dark water.

Margaret stepped into the pond.

The water was shockingly cold. The bottom was slick and silty, just as she remembered from times her mother had walked her in when she was little, before she was strong enough to refuse. She could almost feel it through her shoes, feel the sliding, sucking mud that squeezed between her toes and tried to hold her down.

She took another step, and then another. She was close to the worst part, the drop-off where the pond plunged to unsuspected depths.

Three more steps and Margaret went over the edge. Down she sank through the cold black water. The moon's pale light could not pierce this darkness. And yet somehow she could see. Or perhaps she was guided by the voice, which was calling her more intensely than ever. Not Auntie Alma's voice. The other. She knew who it was, now. But she would not give it a name.

Not yet.

At the bottom of the pond, in darkness black and absolute, she found it. A low mound, features obscured by the silt that had drifted over it in the few days it had been here. She longed to flee. Terror throbbed within her, beating at the walls of her heart, screaming, "Get out, get out, get out!" But the call was too strong, the need of the voice too aching and desperate. Trapped between need and fear, Margaret hung in the freezing water, not certain how much longer she could last here.

The only way out is in.

The words tickled at the back of her mind. She knew they were true, knew they were the only answer.

Moving forward, Margaret reached out to brush the silt from the poor, cold thing at the bottom of the pond.

A lock of hair floated free, and she saw it at last, the face she knew so well, the face she had looked at every morning in the mirror.

Her own face, pale and still in death.

Her wail of despair was lost in the dark water as memory flooded over her, pushing away the lies.

Her parents had not gone off and left her here with Auntie Alma. She had come here herself, running away, hoping to find . . . what? A place to escape, for a time, from the fights—and, even more, from the unbearable hope that they might end, that things might get better, that her mother and father might stop the endless war so they could be a family again.

She had taken the little boat out onto the water, thinking she would be safe, held above the pond, separate from it. Positioning herself in the center of the pond, she had tossed the anchor over the side of the boat. But in her anger and despair she had carelessly managed to tangle her foot in the rope.

The anchor had pulled her under and held her down. She had struggled frantically to free herself, but finally the water had filled her lungs and she had drowned here in the pond's cold, dark embrace.

Calmer now, Margaret studied the pale thing that had

once been her, the body that was hers no longer, and realized that she must have gone backward at the moment
of death, reaching desperately for the world of the living
and refusing to acknowledge the truth of what had
happened.

She had been lying to herself ever since, blocking out
the memory of her death by trying to pretend that her
parents had brought her here, even though she knew in
her heart that the house was empty and that Auntie Alma
had died earlier that year.

No wonder her parents hadn't come for her. How
could they, not having any idea where she had gone?

And now Auntie Alma was waiting on the far
shore . . . one ghost calling to another.

But why am I still trapped here in the water?

Auntie Alma's words sounded again in her head, and
finally Margaret understood. "The only way out is in,"
she whispered.

Beating back her fear, she reached down to embrace
the cold, dead flesh of her body. Wrapping her ghostly
arms around her own corpse, she pressed herself to herself, accepting the reality of her death, rejecting the lie she
had fashioned in her attempt to cling to the world of the
living.

This cold thing *was* her reality, who she was and where she was, and until she accepted that, she could never get through to the other side.

Hard—harder than the night she had tried to press herself into the mattress—she pressed herself back into herself . . .

. . . and burst through the other side.

Suddenly the cold was gone. She felt warm and safe, and light seemed to surround her as she shot to the top of the pond.

Auntie Alma, still waiting on the far side, laughed and applauded when she saw Margaret emerge from the water and climb onto the bank.

Margaret laughed, too—and laughed even harder to find herself warm and dry.

Auntie Alma held out her arms.

Margaret ran to them.

Together, the old woman and the girl walked out of the willows, up the hill, and into the deeper woods, ready to explore the undiscovered country that lay waiting for them on the other side.

The Hardest, Kindest Gift

THREE HUNDRED years ago, when I was only twelve, I sat beside my father's deathbed in a stone cottage near the west coast of France.

I knew that he was absurdly old. Even so, I could not believe he would really die. That childish certainty was shattered when I heard the uncanny wailing outside the window, a heart-piercing keen of despair that seemed to twist and twine around the house, seeping under the doors, through the shutters, down the chimney, and into my very soul.

I burst into sobs and covered my ears. At the same time, my father started up in his bed, his face wild with fear and longing. "That's my mother!" he whispered, stretching out his arms as if to be embraced. A moment later he collapsed against the pillow. I grabbed his hand.

He clenched mine back so tightly that I feared he might break my fingers.

The eerie wailing continued until I thought it would drive me mad. Mercifully, it ceased just before the first rays of the sun crept into the sky. For a time there was a blissful silence, not broken until the full gold of dawn slid across the stone sill and my father whispered, "I will be dead before nightfall, Geoffroi."

I flung myself across his chest, begging him to stay, sobbing out my fear of being left alone in the world. But I could not hold him. By nightfall he was gone, just as he had predicted.

He left me three things: a modest fortune, a life that would be unnaturally long, and a story without an ending.

Of these three things, it was the story, which he told me during his last hour of life, that has most shaped me. In fact it laid hold of my imagination until it became the driving force in my own life for the next two hundred years. For with it came a sense of obligation, and an awareness of a task that I knew I alone was meant to perform.

The idea merely simmered inside me at first. Even when I began to see what I should do I felt helpless, because I had no idea where to start.

It took me longer than it should have to realize that an education would help—as would having enough years added to my face that people would take me seriously. Neither of these things was as simple as it might seem: The knowledge I sought was hidden, and my face did not age at a natural pace. Still, the time came at last when I felt I could begin. In the years that followed, my search led me to stranger places than I had ever thought existed—including, eventually, a small, dusty shop called *La Grenouille Grise,* which was nestled at the end of a narrow street in Paris.

Finding the shop was no accident. Fifteen years of dangerous questions and unlikely contacts had led me to a midnight-dark alley where a cold presence, standing beside me like a shadow, whispered a hint and then disappeared.

That hint was what led me to the shop, though it took another two years to find it.

The proprietress of *La Grenouille Grise* was a gray-haired, gray-eyed, gray-skinned woman who looked as if she, like the items on her shelves, had not been dusted in many years.

"I'm looking for something," I said.

She gestured toward the displays with that attitude peculiar to Parisian shopkeepers, who seem to feel offended by your very presence. Without a word, she was clearly telling me, "Look if you must. But don't expect *my* help!"

Alas, her help was exactly what I needed, as I was fairly certain that the thing I sought was not on display. Risking a bolt of Parisian contempt, I refined my request. "It's something with wings."

I braced myself for her sneer. But the veiled hint had worked. I had at least caught her interest, and she bestirred herself enough to actually point toward one of the shelves.

Turning, I saw a stuffed owl that looked as if it had once been left out in the rain. It was not what I wanted, and she almost certainly knew it.

I shook my head. "What I want would be smaller."

Her expression didn't change.

"And older."

Still no change.

I took my last, best shot. "And still alive."

Her eyes widened by the tiniest degree. In a voice that sounded like the rustle of dry grass in the autumn wind, she spoke the first words she had uttered since I entered: "What is your name?"

"Geoffroi LeGrandent," I said. Then, as if to defy the shame that even after all those years I was not able to entirely hide, I added boldly, "The same as my father."

I caught the slightest flicker of surprise in those ancient gray eyes. She nodded and stood, so rickety and
frail looking that I feared she might collapse before she
could sell me what I wanted.

"Follow me," she wheezed, and shuffled off in a
cloud of dust.

I made my way around the counter—not an easy passage, given the store's clutter. By the time I had picked a
path between the bronze elephant and the display of
cracked pottery, trying to ignore the more grisly relics
(there was something I would have sworn was a shriveled
human hand) she had vanished behind a tattered gray
curtain.

I hurried to catch up with her.

The room we entered was small, dingy, and even
more cluttered than the store. A narrow bed—little more
than a pallet covered by a thin blanket—stood tight
against the far wall. Pointing to it, she said, "Under there."

I knelt. Beneath the bed was a wooden box—oak, I
guessed—held shut with a padlock. I pulled it out, then
followed her back into the store. I placed the box on the
counter.

The proprietress fumbled in her pocket, finally drawing forth a ring of keys. The smallest, needle thin and no
longer than my thumbnail, opened the lock.

I was scarcely able to contain my impatience at her slow, deliberate movements. When she finally lifted the lid of the box I leaned forward eagerly.

Inside was a small glass cube, about four inches to a side. And within that vitrine prison, its ebony wings delicate as lace, fluttered the thing I had sought for so many years.

It was heavier than I had expected.

Far away, at rest in her grotto, Melusine senses that something is happening. She doesn't know what it is, but she can feel it in her veins, the same way she always used to feel it when death was on the prowl for one of her family. She shakes her head, causing her golden tresses to slide over her bare shoulders. That was long ago. These days the bloodline is so thinned she rarely feels that acid premonition, and even then only as a faint, cold tingle.

But this—this is strong. When was it last this strong?

Shall I prepare to fly? she wonders. *After all these years must I take wing once more?*

No. It is not time for that. And she does not want to leave her grotto, this sacred pool that is her shelter and her temple. Not yet. There is still time.

There is always time.

Much too much of it.

The moon rises.

Melusine slides into her pool to swim.

Farther away still, on the hidden island of Avalon, another presence stirs, feeling hope for the first time in thousands of years. . . .

As I left *La Grenouille Grise* with my prize, I thought of my father. How could I not, considering what I carried?

He had been a good man when I knew him. But in his youth he had been a beast. Oh, not in the literal sense; I am not half bear, or boar, or anything like that. In fact, were my father's blood to be truly accounted he would be found one-quarter angel. *Fallen* angel, it is true, though he did have his moments of grace. But it was the fallen part that marked and marred his life, finally driving him to the violent act that had the side effect of toppling the delicately balanced marriage of my grandparents into the realm of tragedy.

That was hundreds of years before I was born. But given the longevity I inherited from him, I have had time enough to piece the story together. Not that it hadn't been told in a thousand forms already. I've read the ones that were written down, and even the most corrupt have at least a grain of the truth at their core. For that matter, I suppose there is no way to know if I have all the truth, either. I say this despite my discovery of my grandfather's testimony, which I alone have read in the last two hundred years. And I say it despite the things my grandmother told me at the end. I have *their* truth, I think. Perhaps that is as close as any of us can hope to get.

Carrying my purchase, I left Paris for the west of France, for the soil in which my family's strengths and sorrows are rooted. It would be my first return in over two hundred years to the cottage where my father died, where I had sat beside him that long, long night.

As I traveled, I read again from the crumbling pages that held my grandfather's story.

Extract from the Testimony of Raymond de Lusignan (as offered to the abbot of the Monastery of Saint-Denis in the year of the Lord 953)

You have asked how I first met my wife. It happened because of what was, to that point, the worst day of my life. I had gone to the forest to hunt with my friend and protector, Count Aimeri of Poitiers. We became separated. While we were apart my friend stumbled across an enormous boar. The beast attacked, and managed to gore the count in the leg.

When I heard Aimeri's scream I raced toward it.
Entering a clearing I saw what was happening and
dashed forward, sword raised. But as I stood above
them and slashed downward, the boar and my dear
friend twisted beneath me. I cried out in horror. My
blade had struck deep into he who had been like a
father to me.

Rage drove my sword again, and I dispatched
the boar in a matter of seconds. At once I dropped
to my knees beside the count and tried to stanch
the horrible wound I had inflicted on him. It was
too deep; no matter how I pressed and held, I could
not stop the flow of crimson life.

Within moments, my friend was dead.

Dropping my face into my bloodstained hands,
I wept until I was senseless.

I do not know how much time passed before I
was able to stand again. When I could, I stumbled
back into the forest, stunned and sickened by what
I had done. I was also afraid for my own life if the
accident should be thought murder when it was
discovered.

In this sorry state I wandered aimlessly for
several days. Then one night, hungry, thirsty, and
half mad, I heard a beautiful voice raised in song.

Following it, I came to a wall of mist. The voice lured me on. Staggering through the mist, I found myself in a moonlit clearing where three maidens danced at the edge of a light-silvered pool. The fairest of them came to ask what troubled me. Though I was afraid to confess what I had done, she somehow eased my fear and the words poured from me like water from a jug.

When I had finished my story the maiden took my hands, which were still brown with the long-dried blood of my friend. They looked strange lying in hers, which were white as milk. She led me into the pool. There she undressed me and bathed me. As she did, the blood and the sorrow and the fear all seemed to wash away together. I felt as if under an enchantment. I suppose it is possible that she was indeed working some spell on me. But I do not think that was the case. I think the only magic was the moonlight, and her tenderness. Or perhaps the only magic was love, for I loved her then as I love her now, all so many years and so many tears later, when I would do anything to take back what happened.

Several miles separated the train station from the cottage. Even so, I made the journey on foot.

I prefer walking when I have a great deal on my mind.

It felt strange to see the old place again. I had kept it all these years with the vague thought that I would some-day return to occupy it. Whether I had not yet done so was because I still wasn't ready to settle down, or because I secretly feared it was haunted, I could not say.

The couple I had hired to care for the place—the current couple, for of course I had gone through many caretakers over the previous two centuries—had done their work tolerably well. The dust was not too thick, nor the windows too grimy.

Though the journey had been tiring, I slept fitfully that night. I tossed and turned, tormented by memories and half expecting to hear a wailing at the windows.

When morning finally came I walked to the remains of my grandparents' castle—nothing now but some bro-ken, moss-covered walls that bore mute testimony to the place's former grandeur.

The forest was not far beyond. It was old and dark and all too clearly haunted—by spirits, I suppose, though I didn't see any of them, but even more by memory and sorrow.

Tomorrow, I told myself. *I'll enter the wood tomorrow.*

In the end it was two days before I found the courage to start this last leg of my journey. When I did, I carried a pack with enough food and water for several days, for I suspected that the way would be long. I also suspected that if I ate or drank anything in the place I was seeking I would never be allowed to leave.

Underneath those supplies, carefully wrapped for its protection, was the glass cube I had purchased at *La Grenouille Grise*.

The trees were ancient, thick, gnarled. Their roots, which rumpled the leaf-covered ground, seemed to reach up to grab my feet as I passed, resulting in more falls than I care to remember.

Unseen creatures moved and muttered in the branches above me and the undergrowth beside me. Mushrooms of an unnatural size, some a sickly blue gray color, others a violent red, grew in clusters beneath the trees.

I could not bring myself, in this forest, to use a hatchet and blaze a trail. I had considered bringing ribbons to tie around branches as markers, but I was fairly certain that when it was time to return I would have found the ribbons missing. Either that, or there would have been a hundred times more than I had originally brought, fluttering in bright profusion for the sake of my bafflement. So I carried a pad and made careful notes and sketches to help me remember my path.

———

It comes closer. Melusine's heart stirs, fluttering like a caged thing trying to escape. Sorrow and memory—which are really the same things for her—rise like a flood, threatening to drown her.

What can it be? she wonders, raising her head to the sky. *Do you know, Mother? Are you watching?*

I know you're still alive, somewhere.

Can't you ever relent?

As I made my way through the haunted forest my thoughts turned, naturally, to my father and his great crime.

Like everything in our family, it had to do with family. His brother, in this case.

Father had had nine brothers in all—nine uncles that I never knew, for all were dead before I entered this world. What I do know, both from Father and from the tales, is that each was stranger than the one who came before, each born with his own curse and his own special gift.

Father was the seventh. He was named Geoffroi, but everyone called him Geoffroi the Tooth, or Geoffroi Big Tooth, or simply The Tooth. This was because of the boarlike fang, bigger than a thumb, that jutted up from the side of his mouth. That was his curse, of course—that, and his ferocious temper.

The gift was his enormous strength. But that combination of strength and temper was a curse in itself. As might be expected, he was both respected and deeply feared in the lands surrounding my grandparents' castle.

Mostly feared.

One day my father and his younger brother, Froimond, got into a fight. No one knew, later, what it was about; some small thing that grew out of all proportion, probably. Terrified of his brother's temper, Froimond took refuge in a monastery.

Driven into a frenzy at not being able to reach Froimond, Father started a fire at the monastery gate. It quickly spread out of control. In the end it burned the place to the ground, killing the abbot and all the monks. A hundred God-fearing men perished in that blaze—a hundred and one, if you count my uncle.

When word of this atrocity reached the castle, it drove my grandfather to speak the words that changed everything.

Memories crowd Melusine's mind more than usual tonight. As she gazes into the pool it seems she can see once more the face of her beloved Raymond.

How long has it been since his death, how many centuries?

How long has she lingered on in this loathsome shape?

How gladly would she lie in the earth at his side if only she could!

She sighs, remembering how she had loved him from the moment of their meeting, first for his tender sorrow, his boylike confusion over the accidental killing of his friend. Then, and more deeply, for the way he looked at her. Last, and most of all, for the unquestioning way he accepted her condition that if they married she must be left to herself on Saturdays, and he must never question why.

No, she thinks now. *Not my condition. The condition set by my vengeful mother.*

She closes her eyes, admitting ruefully that it was her own impulsive act of vengeance that had driven her mother to curse her thus.

Is it in our blood, she wonders, *this thirst for vengeance? Is that what drove my poor son to commit his horrible crime— the blood Geoffroi inherited from me, and I from Mother, fallen angel that she was?*

She corrects herself. *Not was. Is. Eternal and undying.*

She wonders if this fault in the blood is why her mother was one of the Fallen.

But what failed creator is this, who could not make his angels better beings?

Extract from the Testimony of Raymond de Lusignan (as offered to the abbot of the Monastery of Saint-Denis in the year of the Lord 953)

The abbot asks if I didn't realize there was something strange about Melusine. Of course I knew she was different. How could I not? But I was so dazzled with love for her that I willingly accepted her single condition for our marriage: that I must not seek to know what she did on Saturdays. Did this trouble me? How could it not? But her love was so pure and strong that I set my concerns aside. When did mortal man ever have so beautiful a bride—or a better helpmate? I would have been lost without her, for she brought to our marriage both wealth and cleverness, first guiding me as I made my peace with Count Aimeri's family for his accidental death, then as we built our home.

And then she gave me my sons.

Guy was the first, Guy with his startling eyes, one green as the forest, one red as blood. Then his nine brothers, each with his own deformity and his own gift.

At first, love blinded me to their oddities— love for the boys and, even more, my love for their mother. So when the whispers began, the dark mutterings that Melusine had a secret lover and our children carried demon blood, I ignored them. You know how the peasants will talk. Besides, in the six days we had together every week, Melusine was so tender and so true, so attentive to me and to the boys, that I could not doubt her love.

She used to sing to me at night, you know. Her voice was like the sound of a mountain stream. I think that's what I miss most of all. Her singing.

Excuse me. I know, I know, it seems strange for me to weep, even now, even after all this. But it was a happy time.

The last happy time.

My brother was jealous of that happiness. He had found little enough in his own life, despite his wealth, which was far greater than mine, and despite his favored position as firstborn. Perhaps that is why he could not simply be glad for me. Perhaps that is why he worked so hard to poison my mind against Melusine.

No. I must not blame my brother for my fault. Love should have been enough to shield my heart from his poisonous tongue. But his constant whispers, his sneers, his insinuating questions—these things wore away at me as water wears on a rock.

One thing I know: I should never have let him into our home on a Friday night. It was defiant of me, I think—a way of showing I had nothing to hide. But in truth, I had much to hide—not about my wife, but about my own heart, which was tender and raw, harrowed by the doubts he had already planted there. When Melusine excused herself just before midnight all it took was his raised eyebrow, his amused and scornful grin—not even a grin, just a twitch at the corner of his mouth—to drive me to rash action.

In that moment I decided to break my vow to Melusine and spy on her, both to quiet my brother and to set my burning heart at rest.

Near the end of my third day in the forest a light rain— little more than a mist, really—began to fall. I was leaning against a tree to rest when I heard the singing, clear and rippling as water over stone.

I knew at once it must be her.

Following her song, as my grandfather had so many centuries before, I pushed my way through the thickly growing ferns. Rounding a massive tree, I came to a thick wall of fog. I plunged in, certain I had come at last to the place I sought. I stumbled ahead blindly, but after no more than five feet the fog thinned. Soon after that the land dipped, and I found the closest thing I had yet seen to a trail—a little downward twisting path that led between two ever-steepening banks, mostly rocky but dotted with clusters of primrose and eglantine. In the gray light, drops of water stood like jewels on the richly colored petals.

Beneath her singing, enhancing its beauty like a skilled accompanist, was the crystalline music of flowing water.

The rain stopped. The sun, low in the sky, sent shafts of light sideways through the forest, illumining the soft mist from within. The trunks of the trees stood upright within that mist, rising like bars all around me.

The path grew steeper, the banks higher. The light was nearly gone when I tripped, righted myself, and saw her.

Extract from the Testimony of
Raymond de Lusignan
(as offered to the abbot of the Monastery
of Saint-Denis in the year of the Lord 953)

As I have said, every Friday without fail Melusine
retreated at midnight to the tower room she had
claimed as her own. On that fateful Friday I waited
some ten or fifteen minutes after she had climbed
the stairs, then ascended to the room myself, my
way lit by the torches that always burned in the wall
mounts.

Her door was closed. I pressed my ear against it
and heard, faintly, two things: the plash of water, and
my wife, singing. A new flare of jealousy scalded my
heart. Was she singing for someone else?

With the point of my dagger I widened a hole
between two of the door's broad planks. It took
time, for I had to work silently. I had not forgotten
the promise I had made when we married, after all,
the promise that I would not ask Melusine what she
did on Saturdays, or seek to know it in any way. Nor
had I forgotten that she had told me that if I broke
this vow all our happiness must end. But in my
jealous passion it seemed as if all my happiness had

ended anyway. And I kept telling myself that if I could only do this in silence, and if she proved innocent—as some part of me yet believed she would—then she would never know, and all might still be well.

I finished my work and returned my dagger to its sheath. Then I pressed my eye to the hole I had made.

At first I couldn't see anything in the dim light of her chamber. Then my eye adjusted and I spotted her. It was all I could do to keep from crying out in horror. Staggering back, I fled down the stairs as silently as I could.

I did not speak of what I had learned. And when Melusine appeared in her usual form on Sunday she did not act as if she realized I had spied on her. But despite the fact that I now knew she had not betrayed me with any other lover, our happiness was doomed. Oh, my wife had been faithful. But I— I had betrayed her trust completely.

How, then, could love survive?

On the far side of the pool, at the water's edge, sat my grandmother.

I had known what to expect, of course. I had read the descriptions in the legends, in my grandfather's testimony.

It was something else entirely to see her.

From the waist up, she was, even after all these centuries, the most beautiful of women, with abundant tresses of thick, red gold hair that tumbled past her shoulders, flowing like a liquid sunrise over her bare breasts. But at her waist came a grotesque change, for there her body shifted to that of an enormous snake. It was hard to guess the length of this abomination, which coiled beneath her; I imagine it was twenty feet at the least.

Rising from her back, looming over her golden head, was a pair of batlike wings. Even folded and at rest they had a demonic look that I found terrifying.

Her song faltered, then stopped. She stared in my direction. A look of puzzlement crossed her face, then she cried in astonishment, "You can see me!"

After all these years, and even knowing what I would find, I felt as if my tongue had turned to stone. A handful of seconds passed, feeling like a century, before I managed to stammer, "Should I not be able to?"

"It has been a long time since anyone could," she replied. She sounded nervous, uncertain.

"We share the same blood," I said, by way of explanation.

She slid into the pool—the same pool where my grandfather had first met her, first fallen in love with her. The great tail slithered in behind her. To my surprise, she was able to hold her entire torso, as well as several inches of her serpentine lower quarters, above the water. Arms extended, she glided toward me, propelled only by the powerful muscles of her serpent portion.

I thought of what I carried in my pack and felt a moment of uncertainty. Even in this form my grandmother was the most enchanting woman I had ever seen. Now that we were face-to-face, could I really give her what I had spent so long in search of?

He has my mother's eyes, thinks Melusine, staring at the young man who has invaded her clearing.

Those eyes disturb her, for they stir memories of her past—of her mother and the curse she had pronounced as punishment for Melusine's rebellion.

Melusine tries to press back the rising memories of what happened after the night Raymond spied on her and the curse came to its fullness. They flood in anyway, carrying with them all the sorrow and loss of that time.

She had known he had done it, of course—had felt a cold chill in her spine the moment his eye fell on her. But she had not spoken of it, loving him anyway, despite his failure. Perhaps loving him even more for the very humanity of it. And desperately, desperately hoping that if his betrayal remained secret, the doom laid on her might not be stirred after all and they could stay together.

Extract from the Testimony of
Raymond de Lusignan
(as offered to the abbot of the Monastery
of Saint-Denis in the year of the Lord 953)

Here is how my faithlessness was revealed.

In the weeks that followed my spying on Melusine I tried to pretend that it had not happened. Yet the tender closeness we had once enjoyed now seemed forced and stiff.

I have thought about this often in the years since I came here to the monastery, where there is so much time to think, and I wonder if in every marriage there are not things that should remain secret. How much of ourselves can we ever share? Is anyone ready to see the all of it, the deep and secret parts that we ourselves sometimes fear to peek at, much less reveal?

Though I do not have the answer, this much I
now believe: Regardless of what you know, there are
words you should never speak, for once uttered they
can never be taken back, and instead will hang in
the air like a curtain of venom between you and the
one you love.

Thus it was with me and Melusine when we
learned of Geoffroi's crime against the monastery.

From the moment I discovered Melusine's secret
I had begun to think about the boys, of course. It
seemed clear that their strangeness had come
from . . . from whatever she was. I loved my sons
none the less for that. But now I worried about
them all the more. And the whispers that I had shut
out for so many years began to pierce my defenses,
landing like arrows in my heart: "They are demon
seed," the wagging tongues said. "The blood of
Lusignan is tainted forevermore."

Which is why, I confess, when word came
of Geoffroi's atrocity my first, horrified reaction
was not sorrow for the lives lost but shame
for my own family. In a moment of black rage
I turned on Melusine and cried, "Foul serpent!
You have contaminated the blood of a noble
line!"

Would that someone had cut my living tongue from my mouth before I uttered those loveless, heartless words.

Melusine shrieked and bolted from the room. At first I thought that terrible cry, torn from her heart and echoing still in my ears today, was one of rage. All too soon I realized it came from terror.

She ran for her tower. I sprang up to pursue her, but she was faster than I, as she always had been.

She did not go all the way to her chamber. Halfway up the long, winding stair she sprang to the sill of a window and flung herself out.

"No!" I cried, love rising over my anger. *"No!"*

I was but an arm's length behind her. As I clasped the sill to lean out I saw with astonishment that her foot had impressed itself into the solid stone, leaving a deep print. I looked down fearfully, expecting to see her dashed to her death on the rocks below. But a wild cry caught my attention, drawing my eyes upward. What I saw then was worse than my wildest fears could have guessed. My beloved wife, my Melusine, was suspended in midair. Caught between earth and heaven, she writhed and twisted, screaming in agony. Her clothes vanished in a burst of flame. Before my terrified eyes her legs fused into a single thick trunk. It lengthened and lengthened, stretching beneath her in loathsome coils. Blue gray scales slid across its surface, as if she were being sheathed in armor by some invisible smith.

She screamed again. I saw blood spurt from behind her as leathery wings, pointed and demonic looking, ripped their way from her shoulders.

She began to cough. Soon her entire body shook with great spasms, as if she were trying to vomit something forth. At last some small black thing burst from her mouth and fluttered away. Melusine wailed in despair, a sound more heart-wrenching even than her screams of pain, and stretched her arms longingly toward the winged thing. But it quickly flew out of sight.

Only when it was gone did she turn toward me. Her arms were still outstretched, as if she wanted me to take her back, even after what I had done. And her eyes were filled with such anguish that I had my own foot on the sill and was ready to leap into her embrace, heedless of my own life. But before I could make that plunge Melusine was caught as if by an invisible hand and snatched away, vanishing from my sight.

That was the last time I ever saw her. But I heard her again, many times. We all heard her. For she always returned the night before death came to take one of our family. In the midnight darkness she would fly around the castle towers, wailing her warning, until those of us inside were nearly mad with grief.

My grandmother's hooded eyes gazed up at me, the strange vertical pupils only making her beauty more exotic. Then her forked tongue flicked from between her shapely lips, and my fascination turned to horror. Why that one thing above all else should have disgusted me I am not certain. Perhaps it was because in other ways her human and serpent parts were clearly distinct. But that slender tongue darting lightning-like from those human lips made shudderingly real the curse that lay upon her.

"Why have you come here?" she asked. "Why now, after all these years?"

"I have a gift for you."

Eagerness flashed in her strange eyes. But I saw fear as well. As if to hold off the coming moment she turned the conversation, asking softly, "You're Geoffroi's son, aren't you?"

I smiled and nodded, feeling I had reclaimed some pride in my father. "I carry his name, too." I paused, then added shyly, "I heard you, the night you came to wail your dirge for him around our cottage; the night before he died."

She closed her eyes, as if the memory pained her. "Geoffroi was the last of my children," she whispered. "Even so, what I sang was no dirge. It was a cry of desire."

Relief rippled through me, for these words confirmed that I *was* doing the right thing. After a moment I said, "While he was waiting to die, Father told me the story of our family. All but a small part of it."

"What part was that?" she asked, her forked tongue darting out again.

"About your mother."

Melusine looked away, as if gazing into the past, then said softly, "How much do you know? Are you aware that Mother was one of the Earthly Fallen?"

I had learned some about the Earthly Fallen during the years of my quest. Even so, I said nothing, leaving the silence for her to fill, if she was willing.

Pulling herself from the water, Melusine coiled her tail beneath her. Perhaps a foot of her serpent self rose from that coil, its muscular blue gray thickness holding her torso upright, so that her head was actually slightly above mine.

"Mother's name was Pressina. Her downfall came when she refused to choose sides in that most ancient of all wars, the battle that sundered heaven when Lucifer took arms against his creator and shook the foundations of the world." Melusine sighed. "Mother's neutrality provided her no safety. In fact, it proved her downfall, for the Creator demanded absolute obedience and could not stand to look upon those who had refused to take his side. Once the war was over and Lucifer and his rebels had been hurled into Hades, the Creator decided that those who, like Mother, had stayed apart from the battle should be punished as well."

"Why did she stay apart from it?" I asked.

My grandmother shrugged, creating a disturbing movement in the wings that arched behind her. "She understood Lucifer's discontent; indeed, she had felt it herself. But she was unwilling, or perhaps unable, to bring herself to rise against the one who made her. As were many of her fellow angels. In punishment for their neutrality, for not loving him enough, their wrathful creator flung them down to earth. They were oddly out of place in this world, where mortality rules but they themselves could not die."

My grandmother was silent for a time. Though I burned to know her thoughts, I let her sit in peace. At last she said, "They were dangerously beautiful. In time they came to realize that it was safer—safer for them, but even more so for the mortals who surrounded them—to live at the edge of reality as most humans knew it. They drew apart and eventually came to be known as the folk of Faerie. Yet though they kept to themselves, they could not end their fascination with humans."

"Why not?"

She stretched her wings above herself like a dark canopy. "Many reasons, I think. But the most compelling one was that the Fallen—trapped here forever—were fascinated by the ability of mortals to die."

I laughed. "Most of us do not think of that as a gift."

"You have lived far longer than most of your kind, Geoffroi. Even so, you are young. Very young. You mortals think it would be fine to live forever. But there comes a time when it is time to go, when one would welcome death's cold embrace. That's why the Earthly Fallen so often sought to marry mortals, so they could bless their children with mortality." She sighed. "That was the gift Mother tried to give me and that I forfeited."

We sat in silence for a time. Finally I said, "What happened?"

"After many centuries in the mortal realm, Mother married the king of Scotland. She set only one condition upon their marriage: If and when she bore him children, he must not intrude upon the birthing—a condition, one of many, that had been imposed on her kind when they were ejected from heaven.

"Alas, when my sisters and I were being born—all three of us at once—Father was so excited by the news that he broke his vow. He did this not out of jealousy or anger or pettiness, but driven only by his joy, which was our doom. Snatching up the three of us, Mother fled back to Avalon, the island at the edge of the world we know."

My grandmother let the tip of her tail slide into the water. She stirred the pool for a moment then said, "We could have been happy there, if not for the fact that island life feels like a prison when you are young and longing to know the world. When we were fifteen years old, and aflame with restless energy, my sisters and I first learned the story of the life we had lost when our father broke his vow. I was furious at being trapped on that island when we should have been princesses, with all the world to roam in. In my rage I vowed to punish the father I had never known—punish him for his foolishness, and even more for his faithlessness. So with the help of my sisters

I locked him away in the heart of a mountain, in a cell that could not be broken."

She sighed. "Alas, I cast my spells all too well. Though I later repented that rash action, my father spent the rest of his life locked in that darkness.

"Mother, who still loved him despite his broken oath, called us unnatural and vicious children. Her greatest anger was for me, since I was the one who had instigated the act. With flashing eyes she laid her curse upon me."

Melusine paused, and I could tell she was drawing deep from the well of memory. When she spoke again her voice was low, angry, and very powerful.

"'For one full day of every week, from Friday midnight until Saturday midnight, you shall be half serpent. This curse will last until you find a man who proves throughout his whole mortal life that he can do what you punished your father for failing to do: He must never seek to learn your secret. If ever you find such a man, you will be happy, Melusine. But if you wed and that man fails, all happiness will end, and you must take your serpent form forever!'"

Turning away again, Melusine whispered, "That, you see, was the second and crueler part of her curse— crueler even than this hideous shape. For if it came to pass, the mortality she had gained for me by marrying a human would be taken, and I would be doomed to live forever in this beastly form, shunned and feared by all."

I ached for the sorrow in her voice as she told me this, and felt more than ever that I had done the right thing in coming here. Even so, I sensed it was not yet time for my gift. So we continued to talk as the moon rose above the still waters of her pool. Much of what we said then was about my father, last of her children to die, and of his many attempts to redeem himself in the centuries that followed his burning of the monastery.

Finally, as the night was waning, Melusine asked the question I had been waiting for. Putting a hand on my knee she whispered, "Why have you sought me out, Geoffroi? Why now, after all these years?"

"I have brought you something."

Reaching into my pack, I withdrew the glass cube I had worked so hard to find. I unwrapped it slowly, still wondering, despite all she had said, if I was doing the right thing. But my grandmother had seen it, and the hungry look in her eyes reassured me. She extended her hands. Her tongue—which she had tried to keep under control after she realized how it bothered me—flicked eagerly in and out of her mouth.

"Do you know what this is?" she asked, scarcely able to contain her longing.

"It is the thing that was lost to you in the final moment of your transformation."

She loomed above me on the thick muscle of her serpent half, smiling with a sad, brave look that nearly broke my heart.

Inside the glass cube fluttered the small, lost part of her that I had spent so many years tracking down.

Its tiny face was the image of hers.

Without another word Melusine lifted the box and smashed it against a rock.

The glass shattered, freeing her death, which had been born with her, as it is with all mortals. Stretching its lacy black wings, it fluttered up and attached itself to her face.

My grandmother's eyes widened in fear, but only for a moment. Gasping, she breathed in—and in death went. A last cry escaped her lips, a mingled sound of pain and relief, and she toppled to the ground. Her tail straightened, extending far into the pool. It began to thrash, beating the water into a foam.

Like my grandfather before me, I watched in fascinated horror as Melusine transformed—though this was a far different transformation. Her skin withered and wrinkled. The golden hair turned the color of ashes. Her wings crumbled like dry leather, dropping in brittle flakes to the water's surface.

Finally the great tail ceased its lashing.

Soon there was nothing left of Melusine but a scattering of dust—dust, and a blue diaphanous sheath, like that which is left behind when a snake sheds its skin.

Tears falling freely, I carefully rolled up that sheath and tucked it into my pack.

When I finished that task and looked up once more, I was not entirely surprised to see that my grandmother's pool had disappeared. All that was left of our encounter, scattered among the dried leaves at my feet, were sparkling shards of broken glass—the remains of the fragile case that had held the hardest, kindest gift I ever gave.

I thought it was over.

I was wrong. I was still staring at the place where the pool had been when a light appeared in the forest beyond it, moving toward me. From the trees stepped a woman so beautiful that the very sight of her made it impossible to breathe. Her face was young and ancient all at once, and something in her eyes made me look away, for I knew that if I gazed into them for too long I would be lost forever.

A long silence hung between us. I yearned to break it but dared not speak until the woman said, "Do you know who I am?"

As if the question had freed my frozen tongue, I whispered, "You are my great-grandmother, Pressina."

"And do you know why I am here?"

"I do not."

"Look at me, Great-grandson."

I turned my face to her once more and felt a flood of warmth.

"I have come to thank you, as the last thing I do before I leave this realm. I am ancient, Geoffroi—more ancient than you can imagine. And though I am powerful, I am bound by rules more powerful still, rules laid down by the one who created me. Not just rules. Who I am was shaped by who he was, a creator torn between the desire to give freedom and the desire to control—and then, when some of his creations dared to claim that freedom, torn between love and anger." She shuddered. "It was a mighty anger indeed, an anger stronger than love. But love lasts longer than anger, and time changes things, thank heavens. Mountains crumble, continents shift. Even that massive anger, vaster than oceans, harder than granite, has faded with the millennia. Now forgiveness rises in tiny freshets, like the start of a mountain stream. With time and love, ancient curses can be ended, Geoffroi. Time, love, and acts of compassion."

She looked straight into my eyes. "Do you know what you have done for me this night?"

When I shook my head she smiled; I felt as if in doing so she had somehow placed a blessing on my heart.

"I was bound as tightly as Melusine, bound by my own angry act against her—the anger I learned from the one who made me. Parent to child, creator to creation, these things are passed on. As Melusine's mother I wanted—demanded—that she do my bidding, just as *my* creator had demanded unquestioning obedience from we, his angels. And when she did not obey, I foolishly did just as he had done unto me, and cast her out and cursed her."

Pressina gazed around at the forest. In her look I could see a kind of farewell. Turning back to me she said softly, "The stars move. The heavens shift. Anger fades. Slowly, slowly, the need to be all, have all, *dominate* all begins to fade as well."

She extended a hand, not quite touching me yet somehow spreading warmth through every part of my being.

"You have broken not only Melusine's curse, Geoffroi, but mine. Like my daughter, I was bound to this mortal realm until one of my blood was willing to act with courage and love to free me. Now my time here is over at last. Thank you for that, Geoffroi. Thank you."

In less time than the space between breaths, she was gone.

I was alone in the wood.

As are we all.

The Mask of Eamonn Tiyado

HARLEY BURTON stood on the sidewalk at the edge of town, staring along the path that led into the forest. His grandmother had forbidden him to go down there when he was little, and he had never quite gotten over his fear of the narrow, winding trail. Which was why he liked to look at it and imagine what it might lead to. It was a nice piece of mystery in his life.

He was about to turn away and continue toward home when a creaky voice whispered in his ear, "That's where *he* went, the night he disappeared."

Harley spun to see who had spoken. He found himself facing an old woman whose face was so pinched with pain and loss that it almost hurt to look at her. "Who are you?" he asked, backing away.

"Just someone who doesn't want to see you get into trouble." She leaned closer. "I wouldn't go down there if I were you, boy. You might run into . . . him."

"Him?"

She hesitated, as if the words were painful to her, then said, "Eamonn Tiyado."

A prickle of fear rippled over Harley's skin. Every kid in Oak Grove knew about Eamonn Tiyado, the boy who had vanished on Halloween night. It had happened fifty years ago, before most of their parents had even been born. That didn't stop them from using his mysterious disappearance to frighten kids into behaving when they went out trick-or-treating, of course. Grown-ups loved to point to the crumbling mansion at the top of Tiyado Lane and whisper, "That's where Eamonn lived . . . before he got careless." But Harley had never heard that this path was part of the story. He glanced at it and shivered, then turned back to tell the old woman he had had no intention of going into the woods.

She was gone.

Moves pretty fast for an old lady, thought Harley, puzzled. *And what the heck was she talking about, anyway? Crazy old bat.*

He turned to walk on but spotted Annie Dexter heading toward him. She was still a long way off. Even so, there was no mistaking that waist-length, amber-colored hair. Harley sighed. The very sight of Annie made his heart feel like it was twisting inside him. But much as he longed to talk to her, he was all too aware that she was—as his friend Gary phrased it—out of his league. Harley wasn't ugly, he knew that. But he wasn't handsome, either. He was just . . . average. Way too average to get a girl as drop-dead gorgeous as Annie to look at him.

He glanced back at the path, which now seemed more like an escape route. There was no real reason not to go down there. The old woman had clearly been a nutter. And even if there was something scary lurking in the woods, it couldn't be more terrifying than the thought of facing Annie after the way he had made a fool of himself at school today.

He stepped off the sidewalk, onto the path that led down into the forest. He hadn't gone far when he waded into a patch of fog. The mist was lying close to the ground when he first entered it, but before long traces of it swirled as high as his knees, then his waist.

Harley glanced around.

The forest seemed darker than when he had first entered.

"It's just because there are more trees to block the light," he told himself, swallowing nervously. He wondered if he should go back. Annie would certainly have passed the entrance to the path by now, so he could get home without having to face her. On the other hand, for years he had wanted to see what was down here; now that he had finally started along the path he might as well go on for a way. Gary had told him it led to a small lake where the teenagers sometimes went skinny-dipping. Of course, it was too cold for that now. Even so, it would be interesting to see the lake. Harley wondered how far it was.

Fifteen minutes of walking brought him out of the woods and onto a broad shelf of rock that did indeed border a small and quite beautiful lake. To Harley's surprise, on the far side of the lake he saw a cluster of buildings, almost like a little town. It made sense, in a way. Most of the lakes he had been to had had places for tourists to shop. But why had he never seen or even heard of this town, which was so close to home?

He spotted a faint path leading around the lake, and decided to follow it.

The water was still and quiet in the late October afternoon. Brilliantly colored leaves drifted on its surface, touched to fiery brightness by the sun's rays, which came slanting in under a clouded gray sky. The sight should have been lovely. Yet something about it made Harley nervous, as if he sensed currents in the lake that he could not see, much less understand.

Partway around the lake Harley entered a clearing. In its center he saw the crumbled remains of what looked like a stone table. The sight made him shiver, though he couldn't say why. Moving more quickly, he passed through the clearing and back into the woods.

When he came to the group of buildings, Harley was unhappy to realize that most of them were closed. His disappointment eased when he saw that the single store with a light in its window was the most interesting one of all: a magic shop.

How can a town this small support something as interesting as a magic shop? he wondered. Then, with a shrug, he repeated the word his grandmother used to describe all sorts of odd phenomena: "Tourists."

The closer Harley came to the shop, the more fascinating it looked. The mist curled around it like some strange cloud. A large bay window bulged out from the front.

Painted on that window were the words

ELIVES MAGIC SUPPLIES
S. H. ELIVES, PROP.

It was getting darker. Harley knew he should be heading for home, but this was simply too good to resist.

Approaching the door, he pushed it open and stepped inside.

The fact that the shop seemed to be deserted was less important than the fantastic array of items it contained. To his right was a wall filled with cages. He wrinkled his brow in puzzlement. Magicians used rabbits and doves for pulling out of hats. But what were the lizards, toads, and bats for? He started to walk closer, but when the biggest toad smiled at him, he quickly turned away.

The left side of the room was dominated by a glass-fronted counter filled with silk scarves, giant decks of cards, and mysterious-looking wooden boxes.

Stretching across the back of the shop was a long wooden counter with a dragon carved in the front. On top of the counter sat an old-fashioned brass cash register. Perched on top of the cash register was a very handsome stuffed owl.

Behind the counter was a doorway covered by a beaded curtain.

All this was interesting enough. But what really caught Harley's attention was the display at the very center of the store. Under a sign that read PUT ON A HORRID FACE was a table holding a jumble of masks. Harley, who had always wanted a truly scary mask to wear on

Halloween, moved toward it eagerly. The ones carried by the local stores simply weren't that interesting; these looked far better. For one thing, they were the kind that covered your whole head.

The first mask he picked up was a deliciously terrifying werewolf, covered with real—or at least real-*feeling*—fur. Right under it he found a vampire mask with glistening fangs that was horrifying even without being worn over someone's head. Harley touched one of the fangs, and a drop of red liquid oozed out, causing him to shudder even as it delighted him. Continuing to paw through the collection, he found demons, monsters, ghouls, goblins, and ghosts. Then, at the bottom of the pile, he found a mask that, despite being very simple, sent a chill rippling down his spine.

It was the face of a boy about his own age.

Harley could not have said why he found this mask so frightening yet at the same time so irresistible. Plucking it from the pile, he held it in front of him. It had a thick thatch of blond hair, a freckle-dusted snub nose, and a wide, smiling mouth. It was a very handsome face—or would have been, if it had been real. In fact, it was very much the way Harley himself had always wished he looked.

Why, then, did it scare him so much?

Distracted by an odd sound, Harley glanced up. To his surprise, the sound had come from the owl on the cash register. Clearly he had been mistaken when he thought it was stuffed! Blinking at him, the owl uttered a low hoot, then stretched its wings, shook itself, and closed its eyes again.

"Peace, Uwila!" growled a voice from beyond the beaded curtain. "I'm coming."

The curtain parted. An old man, so stooped that he stood scarcely taller than Harley, shuffled out. He had long white hair that hung lank about his shoulders, and wrinkles on his wrinkles. Despite these signs of age his eyes were dark and piercing.

Harley's hands began to shake so badly he dropped the mask.

"Pick that up!" ordered the old man. "Right now!"

His dry, husky voice made Harley think of the wind rustling through the dying leaves of the forest. Quickly, he did as the old man ordered.

The shopkeeper shuffled closer, then smiled, which shifted his wrinkles in odd ways. "Why do you want a mask?"

"For Halloween," answered Harley, thinking it was a stupid question.

The old man stared directly into Harley's eyes. "Tell me the *real* reason."

Harley found unexpected thoughts rising within him: *I want to be someone different. I want to hide my face. I don't want people to know me.*

The words horrified him, both because they were true and because he did not want to utter them in front of this stranger.

"I like disguises," he said at last, somewhat weakly.

The old man nodded. "Halfway to the truth—better than most people manage. All right, which mask did you come to buy?"

"I didn't come to buy anything at all."

The old man shook his head. "No one comes into *my* shop by accident. Now, tell me which mask you want. Quickly!"

Frightened by the old man's ferocity, Harley gulped and said, "I'll take this one!"

The old man—*Mr. Elives?* wondered Harley—looked unexpectedly pleased, almost as if he were relieved. "Fine. That will be two days."

Harley stared at him in astonishment. *"What?"*

"You heard me. You owe me two days. I'll collect them later. Right now darkness is falling and it would be wise for you to move along. Take the side door. It will get you home more quickly."

Seized with sudden panic, Harley bolted in the direction the old man pointed and shot through the door. Time seemed to blur. Before he knew it, he was standing at the top of the path where he had entered the woods.

Harley shook his head. How had he gotten all the way up here? He felt himself blush as he realized he must have been so scared when he left the shop that he didn't even remember running back up the path. But even as he told himself that this was what had happened, he knew it was a lie.

It was only after he had taken his first steps toward home that he noticed he was still holding a mask. Glancing down, he saw with disgust that it was the face of the handsome boy. He sighed. How stupid could he be? With all those wonderful masks to choose from, why had he picked this one? But then, he hadn't really picked it. It was simply the mask he had been holding when he fled the shop.

A tag dangled from the mask's edge. Lifting it, Harley saw handwritten words, the letters formed in a cursive so thin and spidery he had to squint to make them out in the fading October light:

This is the mask of Eamonn Tiyado. It should be worn with care and respect. If it becomes soiled, simply wash with soap and water.

To avoid trouble, we recommend you not wear the mask for more than two hours at a time.

To remove, pinch your nostrils and blow.

A final warning: Do not eat or drink while wearing the mask. To do so is to court disaster!

Harley dropped the tag with a sigh of exasperation. He had bought a mask made by lunatics!

He caught his breath. Had he really "bought" the mask? If so, did that mean he had paid two days for it? And if he had, how were those two days going to be collected?

Sick with fear, Harley continued toward home. When he passed Tiyado Lane he sped up, as if he feared the abandoned house at the end of the street would disapprove of what he carried.

His grandmother was waiting for him in the kitchen, as he knew she would be. She was worried, as he also knew she would be.

"Harley, where have you been?" she signed, her fingers deft and quick.

"Trying to stay out of trouble," he signed back, with complete honesty.

"Well, come on. Supper's getting cold."

Later that night, when he was alone in his room, Harley pulled the mask over his head. It was a bit of a struggle at first; the neck opening was tighter than he had expected and the material did not slide easily over his forehead. But after a moment something changed. He felt the mask grow warm. It began to slither across his skin, moving and adjusting to make a tighter fit all by itself, sealing itself to his skin. He would have cried out in terror—except his mouth seemed to be sealed.

He hurried to the mirror. When he saw his reflection, he did cry out: The mask had adjusted to his face so perfectly it was as if Harley had disappeared, completely replaced by the mysterious Eamonn Tiyado. Even his eyes had changed, from brown to a beautiful deep blue!

Harley clawed at the mask, desperate to pull it from his face. But it felt as if he were tearing at his own skin, and the sudden pain when he dug too hard made him stop.

Looking in the mirror again, he gasped. Scratch

marks had appeared on the mask where he had been gouging at it.

Taking a deep breath, Harley squinched his eyes shut and forced himself to be calm. Finally he remembered that the tag had said something about how to remove the mask. Fingers trembling, Harley put his hand to his neck to search for that tag. To his horror he finally realized it had been sealed under the mask, the only hint of its existence a raised, rectangular patch at the side of his neck.

New panic seized him. The directions had seemed absurd when he read them. Now they were the most important thing in the world. Leaning his head against his dresser, Harley took several deep breaths, trying to bring back the words on the tag. Finally his brain retrieved a phrase: "To remove, pinch your nostrils and blow."

Feeling ridiculous, he tried it.

Instantly, the mask loosened around Harley's neck and ears. Tugging at it, he felt a pulling sensation, almost like peeling dried glue away from your skin. A moment later he was able to lift the whole thing over his head.

Dizzy with relief, Harley flung the mask across the room.

Ten minutes later, when his hands had stopped shaking and his heart was no longer pounding, he went to pick it up. Holding it in front of him, he stared at the lifeless features. Slowly, he began to smile. Now that he knew how to do it, removing the mask wasn't really that hard. Which meant it held intriguing . . . possibilities.

The next day Harley took the mask to school. It was all he could do to keep from showing it to people, but that would have ruined everything. Instead, just after dismissal he slipped into the boys' room and pulled the mask over his face. As before, it sealed itself to his skin, replacing his own plain features with the handsome face of Eamonn Tiyado.

Scurrying out of the school, he caught up with Annie Dexter at the corner of Hawley and Smoot. The sun sparkling in her flowing amber hair took his breath away, and he almost walked straight past, afraid to speak despite the fact that he had a new face to hide behind.

She won't know it's you, he reminded himself fiercely. *Talk to her!*

Gathering all his courage, he said, "Hi!"

Annie looked at him in puzzlement, but he could also see in her expression admiration for his handsome face.

"Hi," she said. "Are you new in school?"

He nodded.

"What's your name?"

The words came out before Harley could stop himself, came from someplace he didn't understand: "They call me Eamonn Tiyado."

Annie looked at him in shock. "That's not funny!" she snapped. Thrusting her thumbs under the straps of her backpack, she turned and stalked away.

Harley watched her go in dismay. Why in the world had he said such a stupid thing?

He began trudging toward home. He had not gone more than a few blocks before an older woman walking toward him looked at his face, then cried out and crossed herself. When Harley stared at her she shook her head, looking embarrassed. "I'm sorry, it's just that I thought . . . but that's impossible. Only . . ." She wrinkled her brow, embarrassment changing to confusion. "You look like someone I went to school with."

Then she burst into tears and hurried on.

Harley ran into the bushes, pinched his nostrils, and got out of the mask as fast as he could.

He did not sleep well that night, his rest plagued by strange dreams of faceless figures chasing him through the forest. The clock beside his bed showed 2:00 A.M. when he got up and moved the mask from his desk to the bottom drawer of his dresser.

The next day, October 30, he took a detour on his way to school so he could walk past Tiyado Lane. Without intending to, he turned onto the street itself. It was short, running only four blocks before ending in a wide circle. On the far side of the circle, behind bent and rusted iron gates, was the driveway that led to Tiyado Mansion.

Harley stood at the gate and looked up. The mansion was perched on top of a hill, almost a hundred yards from the gate. At a display in the town library, he had seen—and admired—pictures of how the place had looked when it was new. It made him sad, now, to see the sagging roof, broken windows, and rotting porch. Once, Tiyado Mansion had been spectacular. Now it just looked . . . tired.

Harley turned and hurried to school, where he was yelled at three times for failing to pay attention.

The next night was Halloween. Harley decided against going trick-or-treating, partly because he thought he might be too old for it, partly because he figured wearing the mask would be pointless, since most people would think he was just some good-looking kid who couldn't be bothered to put on a costume. And anyone who did recognize the face of Eamonn Tiyado would probably freak out the way that woman on the street had.

Instead he went to the community bonfire at the high school. Though he hadn't planned to wear the mask, at the last minute he tucked it into his backpack. Then he kissed his grandmother good-bye and signed that he would see her in the morning, both of them knowing full well that she would be asleep by nine o'clock.

He wasn't sure why he took the mask with him. *Just in case,* was all he told himself. But along the way *just in case* somehow changed to *just for fun* and he decided to put it on.

That was his first mistake. He didn't make the second until two hours later. The bonfire was dying down then. For most of the evening Harley had enjoyed the anonymity that came from having a new face. People looked at him curiously, and though he could often sense a bit of admiration—or envy—for his good looks, for the most part everyone left him alone. The only exceptions to this were a few girls who came over to talk to him. He got the sense that they had been sent on information-gathering missions by their friends, and when he refused to say anything about who he was or where he had come from—he had already learned his lesson in that regard—they retreated to their groups. He was amazed at how much easier it was to talk to a pretty girl when he had a handsome face of his own.

Then he spotted Annie Dexter. He hadn't expected her to be there. Remembering the first conversation he had had with her while wearing the mask, Harley turned to the refreshment table to avoid her. Grabbing a donut, he took a huge bite. As he swallowed, he felt a coldness seize his body. His face began to tingle. He had the terrifying feeling that the mask, already sealed against his skin, was now melting into it.

Only then did he remember the warning on the tag: "Do not eat or drink while wearing the mask. To do so is to court disaster!"

When Harley had read those words, he had thought they were nonsense, a weak attempt at Halloween humor. Now he knew, with sickening certainty, that the warning was vitally important. Rushing from the crowd, he hid in the shadows, pinched his nostrils, and blew.

Nothing happened.

Panic swelling within him, he clawed at the mask.

He would have had better luck trying to tear off his own skin.

And then came something worse, something infinitely worse: A voice in his mind begged, *Take me home! Please, take me home!*

Terror pulsed through Harley's veins. Yet the desperate power of the call was overwhelming. He bolted from the school yard. Without really thinking about it, he ran toward Tiyado Mansion.

The night air was crisp, scented with Halloween magic. Fallen leaves swirled around his feet, and a full moon slipped in and out of the massing clouds. The streets were quiet and mostly empty, though he could hear a band of older boys hooting in the distance. Jack-o'-lanterns still glowed in front of some houses, but most of the porch lights were out, indicating that people were done dispensing candy.

Harley's side ached, and he began to slow his pace.

Take me home! urged the voice in his head again.

Harley ran even faster, driven by the urgency of the words. Overhead he heard the first rumble of thunder. The wind picked up, whipping the leaves across the street and bending the tops of the trees. A few minutes later, gasping for breath, he turned onto Tiyado Lane. Despite the sense of urgency that had driven him here, he stopped in his tracks. Something was wrong. At first he couldn't figure out what. Then, with a shock, he realized that all the cars looked as if they had come from some old movie. Next he noticed that the streetlights were strangely different from the ones he was used to. And the trees! Most of them were smaller than he remembered, and other big trees stood where he had never seen any before.

Lightning sizzled overhead. The world shimmered, and all at once Harley was seeing the street as it looked in the present. More lightning, another shimmer, and the street shifted back into the past.

He would have turned and fled, except the voice, stronger than ever, was still urging, *Take me home! I have to go home!*

More lightning, and Tiyado Lane was back in the present. When Harley reached the cul-de-sac at the end of the lane he slowed down. The towering iron gate that barred the path leading to Tiyado Mansion was closed. He pulled at it. The gate was not locked, but it creaked piteously, barely moving. Another flash of lightning and the gate—straighter and no longer rusty—swung open smoothly and silently.

Home! Home! urged the voice.

The rain began pouring down as Harley raced up the long drive. The mansion loomed above him, its windows flickering, shifting with each bolt of lightning, so first it was all ablaze, then dark and foreboding.

Was the house really moving back and forth through time, or was it simply his vision that kept changing?

At the top of the hill, Harley stopped, panting for breath.

I must go home! Please take me home!

The cry was irresistible. Harley sprinted onto the porch. Without bothering to ring or knock, he pulled open the door.

Standing behind it, as if she had been waiting for him, was the old woman who had spoken to him at the edge of the path the day he got the mask. Lightning sizzled behind him and Harley gasped. Suddenly the woman wasn't old after all, but young and pretty.

Another bolt of lightning, and age reclaimed her.

The voice in Harley's head cried out again, not words this time, just a sound so filled with loss and sorrow that Harley's heart nearly burst with pain.

What did it all mean?

Unable to see because of the sudden tears filling his eyes, he backed away. But before he could turn and run, the woman grabbed his arm. She pulled him into the house, then slammed the door against the mounting storm.

Slammed it, too, Harley felt, against the world he knew and any chance he had of returning to it.

The woman fell to her knees and stared at him. Wiping the rain from his face, Harley could see tears welling in her eyes. She reached out wonderingly to touch his cheek, then sighed. "It's not really you, is it?"

Harley didn't know what to say.

As if his silence gave her hope, she whispered, "Eamonn?"

He shook his head, too fearful to speak.

She sighed again and stood. "Of course not. You couldn't be."

"What's happening?" whispered Harley. "I don't understand."

"This is the last night. I had hoped he would come home."

Harley shook his head. "I don't know what you mean."

The old/young woman smiled sadly. "Nor should you." She glanced at a clock on the wall. "We have a little time. Take off the mask, and I will tell you a story."

"I can't. It won't come loose."

She gasped and put her hand to her mouth. "What have you done to yourself? Never mind. If what you say is true, then tonight is your last chance, too. At least, it is if you want your own face back."

He followed her through the house, which continued to shift with each lightning flash, one moment well kept and orderly, the next a cobweb-festooned horror of peeling wallpaper, sagging ceilings, and buckled floors. When they came to the kitchen she motioned for him to sit at a long table.

She took a chair opposite him. Staring straight into his eyes, she said, "I don't know who you are, or where you found that mask, but I'm glad you've come. It was the only chance for Eamonn. And now it seems that I am the only chance for you. So we'll have to work together."

Harley started to ask a question, but the woman shook her head. "Just listen."

A flicker of lightning showed through the window and the suddenly beautiful woman sitting across from him began her story.

"I was born in the mountains of central Europe. When I was in my early teens, my parents married me to an artisan, a man who made masks for royalty, for the court balls. I did not complain at their choice, in those days we did as our parents told us. Besides, he was very handsome, with dark flashing eyes and clever hands. But there was something hard and hidden in his heart, and he could be cruel as well as kind. But still I loved him. Loved him deeply.

"During the second year of our marriage my husband began to disappear without explanation. At first it was only for days, but as time went on his absences grew longer and longer. After each absence he would return with many masks, so I assumed he had been working. Even so, I wondered if he had another woman. Jealousy began to eat at my heart. Finally I decided to follow him on one of these trips." She shuddered. "That was how I learned about the Faceless Ones."

"The Faceless Ones?" whispered Harley, fearing the answer but needing to know.

Lightning flashed outside the window. Once again she was the haggard crone Harley had met at the edge of the woods.

"The Faceless Ones were my husband's victims. They were—had been—people born with great beauty but weak character. Or perhaps their character was weak *because* of their beauty, because it made life too easy for them. In any event, they were my husband's natural prey, and he was able to bring them under his power and steal their faces."

Harley shivered. Against his will, his fingers crept to the handsome face now covering his own plain, pudgy features.

"He stole their faces then sold them as living masks to men and women who were rich and royal but hardly fair of feature. The customer would go off on a journey ugly and months later return home with not only a new face but a new name, telling some story about being the favored first cousin—and heir—of the rich and royal man or woman who had died tragically while traveling abroad.

"For years my husband sold these masks and made a great deal of money in doing so. But as his victims grew in number, so did our danger."

"Why?" asked Harley.

"Because they did not die from their loss. Instead they lived on, lurking in the shadows. Waiting." She glanced away for a moment, then said slowly, "As the numbers of the Faceless Ones grew, they slowly found each other and vowed to work together for their revenge. They did not dare appear in the daytime, of course. But at night they were always waiting just outside the light—waiting for us to stumble into their hands.

"In time the danger grew so great that my husband decided we should flee Europe. We had plenty of money, for his customers had paid him dearly for the 'masks' that changed their lives. We came to this country, leaving behind—we thought—his faceless victims, those shadow people who lived in loss and misery.

"Finally we settled in this town, which seemed like a good place to be forgotten. We changed our name to 'Tiyado,' built our home, had our son."

Harley felt a shudder ripple down his spine. "Eamonn?" he whispered.

She nodded. "Yes, we called him Eamonn, and he was the joy of my existence. For a time the three of us lived in perfect happiness. Then one night I saw a figure lurking outside our home and knew with horrid certainty that the Faceless Ones had followed us. It had taken them years, and the lord alone knows how they did it, but they had chased us and traced us, and now they were on our doorstep.

"For months we lived in terror. At last, despite my pleas and my tears, one Halloween night my husband went to talk to them. 'What do you want?' he asked.

"And they told him."

She turned away, her shoulders shaking with sobs, and Harley suddenly knew what the Faceless Ones had demanded as their revenge. "They asked for Eamonn's face, didn't they?" he whispered.

The old woman answered without turning back to him. "I begged my husband not to do it. I told him we could flee again, find a new place to live. But his heart was hard, and he had never loved the boy anyway, not as a father should. He knocked me out and tied me up, and when I woke, my husband and my son were gone. My husband came back. My son did not. And my husband was never my husband after that. *Never.*"

"And you never saw Eamonn again?" asked Harley.

"No, I saw him often. He lived in the woods with the other Faceless Ones. I took him food and clothing. But

I never saw his beautiful face again—not until tonight, when you appeared at my door wearing it." Turning back to look at him directly, she whispered, "Eamonn lost his face fifty years ago tonight. This is the last chance, the last chance for him to get it back. I had been praying for some miracle to appear. I wasn't expecting . . . you."

Another flash of lightning lit the room and she was once more young and beautiful. "Come," she said, taking his hand. "Come with me! It's your last chance, too. If you cannot return Eamonn's face, you will never see your own again, either. You will be wearing his for the rest of your life!"

They raced out of the house and into the darkness, the old/young woman and the boy with the face that was not his own. The rain drenched them, the wind battered them. They flickered in and out of time with each bolt of lightning as they pelted through the town to the edge of the forest, then down the little-used path until they came at last to the shore of the secret lake.

A little farther and they reached the clearing where Harley had seen the crumbled stone table. Only now the table was whole and solid, and bound to its top was a boy with a handsome and very familiar face: Eamonn Tiyado.

Crowded around the table were dozens of the most horrifying people Harley had ever seen: men and women who were . . . blank, as if their faces had been wiped away, leaving only their eyes, a pair of holes for their noses, and gaping, toothy voids where mouth and lips should be.

At the head of the table, looming above the boy, was his father, wielding a knife that shimmered with silver magic.

The Faceless Ones moaned and swayed, waiting for the mask maker's glowing knife to fall. Eamonn's mother cried out in fear and horror.

Then the lightning flashed, and they were in the present once more. The table was gone, only a tumble of stones left to mark where it had once stood.

Harley heard a moan from behind them and turned. A faceless man shuffled out of the trees, a living nightmare who pricked Harley's heart not to fear but to sympathy.

Harley waited for another stroke of lightning, but it did not come.

They were trapped in the present.

"Eamonn Tiyado?" he whispered.

The man moaned and started toward him.

The old woman uttered a piercing cry, the sound of a broken heart breaking yet again. Then the lightning flashed, and they were in the past.

Harley hoped, for a breathless moment, that they could somehow intercede and change what had happened. But it was too late. Eamonn's father was holding the boy's face in the air, and the Faceless Ones were thumping their approval.

The sight drove Harley to an anger unlike anything he had ever known before. "No!" he screamed. "Noooo!"

The Faceless Ones turned in his direction. At the same time, Eamonn's mother grabbed Harley's arm, crying, "Run! Run!"

Harley shook her off. Stooping, he picked up a stone and flung it with all his strength. As if guided by heaven itself, it struck the mask maker's knife, which exploded in a shower of blue and silver sparks.

The mask maker clutched his smoking hand, screaming with both fury and pain, then backed away as the Faceless Ones turned on him, surging forward.

"Get back!" he cried in horror, putting up his hands to ward them off. "Get back!" But his pleas were lost in their combined moans, and a moment later he fell beneath their relentless tide.

Then the lightning flashed and Harley was in the present once more.

The storm was abating now, the rain little more than a light drizzle, the thunder a distant rumble.

The man Eamonn Tiyado had become staggered forward, reaching out hands that trembled with longing. It took every ounce of courage Harley had to not bolt back up the path. But he stood still, waiting.

The shambling creature stopped in front of him. The blank, smooth face was horrifying. But the eyes . . . Harley knew those blue eyes. He had seen them in his own mirror, the first time he put on the mask.

Eamonn Tiyado reached toward Harley's face. The boy had to resist the urge to lurch away as the faceless man placed trembling fingers behind his neck. He scarcely dared to breath as Eamonn's fingertips pressed against his flesh.

He felt a sudden pull on his skin. The mask fell away, dropping into Eamonn's hands as easily as if it had been attached by nothing but a flimsy string.

As it did, a piece of paper fluttered to the ground.

Harley ignored the paper, watching eagerly as Eamonn Tiyado lifted the mask of the beautiful boy, the face of his own childhood, and stared at it hungrily. Then, with a sigh so low it might have been a moan, he pulled it slowly over his head.

The old woman standing beside Harley clamped her hand on his shoulder. He could feel her shaking. Together they watched as the mask wrapped around her son and . . . shifted. The features stretched and extended until they were no longer those of a boy, but those of a man of about sixty. Finally they settled into a face that was ravaged by loss and sorrow, yet still handsome for all that.

Tears shimmering in his eyes, Eamonn Tiyado leaned close to Harley. "Thank you," he whispered.

Harley lifted a hand to his own face, his pudgy, normal face, and felt a sense of relief so powerful he could barely keep from screaming out his joy. "It was my pleasure," he said.

Looking down, he noticed the piece of paper that had fluttered loose when he handed the mask to Eamonn. He had assumed it was that tag, the one with the instructions he had so unwisely ignored. He stooped to pick it up, thinking it would make a souvenir of his adventure. When he looked at it he was surprised, but only slightly, to see that the words had changed. Now they said simply:

Two Days: PAID IN FULL!
—S. H. Elives

Herbert Hutchison in
the Underworld

HERBERT HUTCHISON was fifteen when the car he was driving hit a patch of black ice.

This was a bad thing, for several reasons. First, he was too young to have a driver's license. Second, the car was his mother's, and he had taken it without permission. Third, he was already due to appear in court the following week on a petty theft charge. Fourth, he was slightly drunk at the time. Fifth—and possibly worst, from Herbert's perspective—he was going about 80 miles per hour when it happened.

The fact that there was a solid rock wall on one side of the road and a deep chasm on the other did nothing to improve the situation.

Herbert managed to hit them both, bouncing off the rock wall with a crash and squeal of metal, then back across the road, where his still-speeding vehicle shot through the guardrail and hurtled a good ten feet straight ahead before it began its (very rapid) descent.

"Oh hell!" was all Herbert had a chance to think before the car hit the rocky slope, rolled over three times, then exploded in a ball of orange and yellow flame.

Still, it was an appropriate thought, as hell was indeed Herbert's next destination.

It took Herbert a while to realize that he was dead. For one thing, he was in a lot of pain, which, to him, seemed to indicate being alive. For another thing, he had always been a very lucky person. So the idea that he might have survived even as spectacular a crash as the one he had just created didn't entirely surprise him. After all, he had spent a lifetime avoiding serious consequences for major problems of his own making. So the idea that he had escaped yet again didn't seem that far-fetched.

Two things worked together to change Herbert's mind. The first came when he glanced behind him and saw the still-fiery wreckage of his mother's new car. *Whoa!* he thought. *Did I really manage to walk away from that?* Still, he might have been able to convince himself he had survived even *that* spectacle of destruction, if not for the second thing, which was that the earth opened beneath his feet, dropping him into a long, black tunnel.

That was when he was sure he was dead.

Herbert had no idea how long his fall lasted. It seemed like forever. Again, there was more than one reason for this. First, he was impatient by nature, so everything seemed to take forever. Second, he was still in excruciating pain.

He had time to examine himself as he fell. His clothes were torn and bloody, but not singed. Had he been thrown through the windshield before the car erupted in flames? That would certainly explain the throbbing pain in his head and the blood dripping down his face, not to mention the deep gashes in his chest. From the way his right arm was hanging, Herbert was pretty sure he had broken it. He pulled aside his torn sleeve for a closer look and screamed.

The jagged end of bone sticking through his flesh confirmed that the arm was indeed broken.

He finally landed, with only the mildest of thumps, on a path lined with primroses. He didn't know they were primroses, of course, having studiously resisted his mother's efforts to share her joy in gardening. But he did recognize them as something that had once grown beside his house.

Beyond the primroses the underbrush was dense and looked impassable. Erupting from that tangle of bushes and vines were broad tree trunks, regularly spaced. Herbert looked up. The branches crisscrossed over the path, twining around each other to form a dense canopy about five feet above his head. It was like being in a tunnel made of plants.

Herbert turned to look behind him. The path that way was blocked by a solid hedge. He might have tried to push his way through it, if not for the fact that the vines sprouted thousands of two-inch thorns that actually glistened in the low light.

Where was the light coming from, anyway? Herbert looked in all directions but could see no source for it.

He sighed. Clearly this tunnel only went one way.

Limping, trying not to scream, he started forward.

Herbert had no clue how long he had been walking— given the pain he was in, it felt like an eternity—when the green tunnel widened and he saw a sheer cliff rising ahead of him. This would have been the end of his journey, save that at ground level it was pierced by an arched opening. Carved above that opening were the words ABANDON HOPE, ALL YE WHO ENTER HERE.

Two creatures stood guard. Though Herbert's mind

resisted the idea, their horns, tails, pitchforks, and flame red skin made it clear that they were demons.

He turned to go back. But though he had traveled for what seemed like hours, the wall of glistening thorns was still only five feet behind him.

Herbert was ready to abandon all hope even *before* he passed through that arch, something he was clearly meant to do, when a voice to his right whispered, "Herbert! Herbert, come here!"

He blinked and glanced around.

"*Over here!*" whispered the voice urgently.

Herbert stepped to his right. Though the underbrush was too thick for him to leave the path, he could see a glowing Being just beyond it. He couldn't make out its features. Even so, the very sight of it somehow eased his heart.

"What do you want?" he whispered.

"I'm hoping you can do me a favor."

"What?"

Despite the thickness of the undergrowth, the Being stepped through it with no problem. Herbert had a sense of light, of freedom, of wings, of music. His sorrow faded, and he felt an inexpressible longing. "Who are you?" he asked.

"A messenger."

"You have a message for me?" Herbert's heart lifted with fresh hope. He was going to get out of this after all!

The Being laughed, but it was not a mean laugh. "Not for you," it said. "For . . . *him.*"

The way it said "him" made Herbert shudder.

"Look, I'm in an awful hurry. And the truth is, I don't really like to go in there. If you could just take this box to *him* I would deeply appreciate it."

"What will you give me if I do?" asked Herbert shrewdly.

The Being seemed startled. Then it smiled, though how Herbert could have known this, since he still couldn't see its face, he wasn't quite sure.

Reaching out, the Being placed its hands on either side of Herbert's head. To Herbert's astonishment, the throbbing pain that had been with him since the accident vanished. Next, the Being slid its hand down Herbert's arm. The boy heard an odd sucking sound—the jagged edge of bone pulling itself back inside his skin.

"Wow," he breathed. "Thanks!"

"My pleasure," said the Being. "Literally. I love to heal. Anyway, in return, please take this to . . . *him.*"

"How will I find, um, *him*?"

The laugh this time was like tinkling bells. "Oh, you

won't have any choice about that! Once you're here, all roads lead to . . . well, you know who."

"Can't you take me back with you?" asked Herbert.

The Being shook its head. To Herbert's surprise, he could feel its sadness. "No, that's not possible. Still, do this thing for me and you'll have a friend on the other side. Oh, one more thing, Herbert."

"What?"

"Please don't open the box."

"Okay."

"I'm serious. Whatever you do, don't open the box!"

"Sure, sure."

Herbert had always been easy with a promise.

"I'm very serious about this," persisted the Being.

"So am I!" said Herbert, who was always offended when anyone doubted his word, no matter how many times he had lied to that person in the past.

"All right. Good luck!"

The Being shimmered and vanished.

Herbert stood for a moment, examining what had been placed in his hands. It was a plain wooden box, dark brown, highly polished. Its hinged lid was held shut by a simple brass latch. The latch didn't even have a lock. Herbert shook his head in amazement. How trusting could someone be? Well, the Being—obviously an angel—had been good to him. He wouldn't open the box.

At least, not yet . . .

Tucking the thing under his miraculously healed arm, reveling in the fact that the pain was gone, Herbert started toward the stone arch.

Given where he was, he felt oddly hopeful.

Though Herbert had expected the demon guards to stop him, they simply yawned and nodded and said, "Yeah, yeah, go on in."

Herbert stepped forward and ran into an invisible wall.

The demon on the right shook his head. "Geez, kid, can't you read?"

"Huh?"

The demon pointed up. "The sign. The sign over the door!"

"Yeah, I read it."

"Well, then empty your pockets."

"Huh?" he asked again.

"You sure you read it?" asked the demon on the left.

"You sure you *can* read?" snickered the demon on the right.

With a roll of his eyes, Herbert looked up. He let out a low groan. He had misread the words the first time. Either that or they had changed somehow. The carving now said ABANDON DOPE, ALL YE WHO ENTER HERE.

"Come on," said the demon on the right, holding out a scaly red hand. "Fork it over."

"Fork it over!" cried the demon on the left, flicking out his forked red tongue. "Fork it over! Flaming farts but I love it when you say that."

Herbert shook his head. If this was what passed for humor around here, he really was in hell. With a sigh he dug in his pocket and pulled out the joint he had been on his way to share with a friend before his untimely death.

"All right, you can go in now," said the demon on the left, plucking the joint from Herbert's hand. He touched the tip of the white roll with his finger. Instantly, smoke began to curl from the end. He passed it to his partner, who took a puff and smiled and said, "Ahhh." He winked at Herbert. "Good shit, kid. Thanks."

Herbert Hutchison sighed, and entered the underworld.

At first hell didn't seem that bad. He was in a broad stone tunnel that sloped gently downward. It was a trifle warm, perhaps, but he had always liked hot days at the beach. The red light, which came from holes in the rocks— sometimes above him but just as often from the side— was beginning to bother him. And the occasional scream of agony that echoed down the corridor was somewhat unnerving. But the thing that bothered Herbert most was the box he was carrying, and the fact that he was not supposed to open it.

It was hard to keep track of time, so he wasn't sure how long he had been walking—long enough to get fairly tired—when he came to a place where a small cave opened to his right. Glancing around, Herbert ducked into it. Even though he had not actually met anyone else in the tunnel, it seemed safer, somehow, to rest here than in the tunnel itself.

As he sat, he studied the box. The fact that it wasn't locked was driving him nuts. He wondered if he would get in trouble if he did open it. Then he laughed. "I'm in hell already. How much more trouble can I be in than that?"

With practiced fingers—the fastenings were not unlike those of his mother's jewel box, from which he had frequently stolen money—he opened the lid and looked eagerly inside.

"Oh crap," he muttered.

Inside the box was . . . another box. Herbert took it out and studied it for a minute. It was exactly like the first box, except smaller.

Well, there was one difference. Unlike the first box, this one seemed to carry a slight electric charge.

"My Spidey sense is tingling," he said, amused at his own wit.

Even so, he put the small box back, then carefully closed the lid of the larger one.

After a while Herbert got bored with sitting and started to walk again.

Eventually the tunnel opened onto a ledge on the side of a steep slope. Far below stretched a broad plain that ended at the shore of a mighty river. The river itself was blanketed by swirling mists.

Above the plain flew creatures that—given their muscular red bodies and batlike wings—could only be more demons. Unfortunately, these were far more terrifying than the ones he had already met.

Herbert shuddered. This was getting serious!

His thoughts were interrupted by a small voice saying, "Well, kid, what are you waiting for?"

Herbert looked down. Standing next to him, only knee high, was a *cute* version of the horrifying creatures soaring over the plain. It was holding a foot-long pitchfork.

"What are *you*?" he asked.

The creature rolled its eyes. "Boy, I can see you've got a lot to learn. I'm an imp!"

Then it poked Herbert in the leg with the pitchfork.

"Ow! Don't do that!"

"Then don't ask stupid questions."

"My teachers said there was no such thing as a stupid question," said Herbert self-righteously.

"Do you see your teachers anywhere around here?"

Herbert shook his head.

"Then don't ask stupid questions! What's in the box?"

"Don't ask stupid questions," said Herbert smugly.

"And don't be a smart-ass," snapped the imp, running behind Herbert and jabbing him in exactly that spot with his pitchfork. "It's a bad idea. Besides, that wasn't a stupid question."

"All right!" shouted Herbert. "Just don't do that again. What's in the box is . . . another box."

"Don't give stupid answers, either!" snapped the imp, stabbing at him again, this time in a more private place.

Herbert managed to dodge the jab, much to his own relief. "It's not stupid," he said. "It's the truth. Here, I'll show you."

He opened the box.

The imp stepped closer, peered inside, then rolled its

eyes again. "Okay, so it's another box. What's inside *that* one?"

Herbert shrugged. "I'm not supposed to open it."

The imp laughed. "And that's how you got *here*, right? By always doing what you were supposed to?"

Herbert felt himself blush.

"Oh, forget it," said the imp. "You're not worth my time."

And then it vanished.

Herbert, annoyed, did the only thing that made sense to him at the moment.

He opened the box.

Inside was an envelope.

Written on the envelope, in the most perfect, flowing cursive Herbert had ever seen, was his own name. He felt a sudden clench of fear. What was this about? What was in the envelope? And why was he supposed to take it to . . . *him?*

He stood, wracked with indecision, longing to open the envelope, but frightened, too.

"Hey, kid!" snarled a voice from above him. "Get moving!"

Looking up, Herbert saw one of the large demons hurtling toward him, fiery eyes blazing. With the same practiced speed that had saved him from his mother so many times, he snapped shut first the smaller box and then the larger one. Then he started down the path.

Satisfied, the demon soared upward again.

It took Herbert hours to make his way to the base of the mountain, and hours more to reach the edge of the river. He knew that was where he was supposed to go because every time he tried to head off in any other direction one of the demons would swoop down, pitchfork raised and ready for jabbing, to steer him back the way they wanted him to go.

Herbert couldn't help but notice that it was growing hotter. Also, an unpleasant smell was starting to burn his nostrils. He might have been more disturbed by these things if he hadn't been so consumed by wanting to know what was in the envelope. The problem was, he didn't dare open it while the demons patrolled above him.

He had only been standing at the river's edge for a few moments when a boat loomed out of the mist. Its prow, from which hung a glowing lantern, slid onto the rocky bank without a sound. At the back of the boat stood a cloaked figure, its face hidden by a large hood. It raised one spectral hand and beckoned toward Herbert.

The boy backed away—and bumped into something

hot. Turning, he saw that two demons, each about eight feet tall, had landed behind him. Their wings rose in high, jagged points over their shoulders. Their eyes were like holes into another world, one where fires raged. Their muscles bulged in a way that made the superheroes Herbert liked to draw when he was supposed to be doing homework look scrawny.

With a sigh, he climbed into the boat.

The boatman pushed on a pole, and they left the shore. Soon they were enveloped in swirling mists. They had traveled in silence for some time when the boatman asked, in a voice that seemed as if it came from the bottom of an empty grave, "So, kid—what's in the box?"

"I don't know," said Herbert miserably.

The boatman uttered a mocking laugh that made Herbert burn with shame and fury. Did the boatman think he was a fool for not opening the box? He almost asked, but his thoughts were diverted by a terrible sound from ahead of them. It took Herbert a moment to realize what he was hearing: thousands of voices, wailing and moaning in agony.

"Ah," murmured the boatman, "we're almost there!"

Turning away, he began to guide the craft ashore.

This is it, thought Herbert desperately. *My last chance. If I'm going to see what's in that envelope, I'd better do it now!*

But the angel asked me not to, argued another part of his mind.

Screw the angel! snapped the first part. *He didn't even have the guts to come down here and deliver the damn thing himself. He could have made the trip in a tenth of the time it's taken me so far. Who died and made me his errand boy, anyway?*

The wailing was growing louder. Herbert had to know what was in that envelope. Maybe it offered some hope of escape!

He glanced up. The boatman was still facing ahead, guiding the boat into place.

Quickly, despite the trembling in his fingers, Herbert opened the first box, and then the second.

He took out the envelope.

It wasn't even sealed! He could read it, and no one would even know! How stupid was that?

Unable to resist a smile, he opened the back flap of the envelope. Ignoring the thump of the boat against the shore, he took out the message and began to read:

Dearest Herbert,

Oh, my dear boy, we are so very sorry! Because we are a god of mercy, it is our policy to offer hope until the very last moment, no matter how bad someone has been in life.

In fact, we give three chances.

Alas, Herbert, you failed all three times. Even after opening both boxes, had you delivered this envelope unopened, we would have been able to retrieve you from the one in whose realm you now stand.

As it is, you now belong to him.

We sincerely wish it could have been otherwise.

Love,

The Almighty

"That's not fair!" wailed Herbert.

"No one said life was fair!" replied a gravelly voice. With a horrible laugh, it added, "And death is even worse!"

Herbert looked up, straight into the glowing eyes of the biggest demon he had seen yet.

It smiled, revealing a mouth full of truly terrifying fangs.

And that was when the pain really began.

The Boy with Silver Eyes

THERE is always one unicorn on Earth, come as a reminder of what the world has lost. This is an ancient promise, made by the unicorns after they fled to Luster because the Hunt for them on Earth had become so savage they feared they could not survive.

There is always one unicorn on Earth, who risks his life by returning so we will not forget the sweetness and the magic that were once our birthright.

There is always one unicorn on Earth, who comes to spend twenty-five years as the Guardian of Memory, the sweet reminder of what we once had.

Alas, this unicorn does not always survive that service.

This is how it was with Streamstrider, who liked to dance on water and could prance across a river on the

206 • BRUCE COVILLE

tips of his hooves. At least, he could until the day a
Hunter's arrow found his heart.

A shiver ran through the unicorns of Luster when
Streamstrider fell, for they always know, at once and
without question, when one of their own has died. The
queen, Arabella Skydancer, wept the most bitter tears of
all, for it was she who had given the pledge to send a unicorn back to Earth. Though she had known when she
made the promise that it was not without danger, it still
pierced her own heart like an arrow every time that price
was paid.

The Hunter who had slain Streamstrider cut off the
glimmering horn and took the trophy to the woman
called Beloved, who was the leader of the Hunter clan
and the ancient enemy of all unicorns. She clutched it to
her chest and crooned with delight that another of the
foe had fallen.

And then the Hunter did something else, something
no Hunter had ever done before and none has dared do
since. He skinned the carcass and cut up the meat, which
he took home to feed his family—his wife, Therese, and
his son, Nils, who was but four years old. But Therese
would not touch the meat, for though it sizzled tantaliz-
ingly on the spit, the smell of it—a smell of clear water
and mountain breezes, of fresh spring grass and flowers

not yet open—was strange, and it frightened her. Nor did Nils want to eat, for he saw his mother's fear, and it made him afraid as well. But the boy feared his father's wrath even more, and when the Hunter raised his fist and roared, "You'll eat, by God, or I'll know the reason why!" Nils put a piece of the meat to his lips.

When the Hunter saw this he was satisfied, and cut a huge chunk of the unicorn meat for himself. Silvery blood ran over his chin as he crammed the gobbet into his mouth. But he was a hasty man, and he chewed only two or three times before he tried to swallow. The meat lodged in his gullet, and he began to choke. Eyes bulging, he clutched at his throat. No sound came from his open mouth.

Nils watched in terror as his mother screamed and pounded on his father's back. Her efforts were of no avail; moments later the Hunter lay on the floor, his face blue, his chest unmoving.

Only then—and mostly because he did not know what else to do—did Nils swallow the piece of meat he had been holding in his own mouth.

In that moment he was changed forever.

Nils and his mother lived in a cottage at the edge of the great northern forest. Though they were far from rich, they did not want for any of the necessities of life. In part this was because Therese was a skilled gardener and seamstress. But it was also because Beloved sent Therese a small bag of gold every year, as token of her appreciation for what her husband had done. And, though the two did not know it, other Hunters kept watch on the cottage, to make sure they remained safe.

After the first year, Therese did not say anything to Nils about the gold. This was because the one time he saw it he shrieked in horror and fled the cottage, and it took her seven hours to find him.

Despite being safe and having enough to eat, Therese did not rest easy, for two things gnawed at her heart. The first was sorrow for her lost husband, who had been gruff and demanding but also a cherished companion. The second was Nils, who grew stranger and more dreamy with every passing month. Something in the boy's eyes when he gazed into the woods troubled her. Even worse were the days when he sat at the side of the cottage staring into the forest and singing wordlessly to himself—a song so filled with longing that it made his mother weep, which was something the boy himself never did.

Sometimes she would sit down beside him and ask, "What are you looking for, Nils?"

"I don't know," he would whisper. "Something. I want *something*, Mother. But I don't know what it is."

These were strange words to hear from a boy who was but five years old, and they troubled Therese greatly.

Once, he woke her in the middle of a rainy night, saying, "Listen! *Listen!*"

"It's only the rain," she said, caressing his golden hair.

"No, not the rain. The voices *in* the rain. What are they saying? I can't understand them!"

When Therese told Nils there were no voices, at least none that she could hear, his eyes grew wide and he crawled into bed beside her, where he spent the rest of the night shivering in terror.

Despite these things, much of the time Nils was one of the happiest creatures in all the north. This was partly because he loved the great forest behind their home and spent most of his hours playing there.

At first his love for the forest worried Therese, who feared he would get lost in the deep strangeness of the place. When the boy was still little she tried putting him in a sort of harness and tying him to a tree so he could not wander more than thirty feet away. The first time he escaped from the harness—he was six, and she never did figure out how—she was seized with panic and she plunged into the forest in search of him. She had been looking for over an hour when he ambled up to her, seeming surprised to find her so upset. When she snatched him up he patted her cheeks with his little hands and crooned, "Don't cry, Mama! Don't cry!"

"Where have you been?" she demanded, anger and relief mixing in her voice.

"Looking for something."

"Looking for what?"

Trouble clouded his eyes. "I don't know," he said sadly, twisting in her arms so he could stare back into the forest. "There's something my heart needs to find. But I don't know what it is."

Therese carried him back to the cottage, her heart pounding, though she could no more say what she was afraid of than Nils could tell her what he had gone in search of.

Another time he frightened her by running into the cottage and crying angrily, "The eyes under the bushes won't come out and play with me!" When she tried to get him to tell her what he meant, all he would do was point at the bushes near the edge of the woods and howl, "There! There! The eyes under the bushes."

"What do they look like?" she asked tenderly, her heart breaking with sorrow for his sorrow—and with fear that he was mad.

"I don't know," he whimpered. "All I can see is their eyes."

As for Nils's own eyes, they came to be a matter of some discussion in the village, for as he grew older they turned—so slowly that none could say when it happened, but as surely as the changing of the seasons—from blue to silver. Eventually "the boy with silver eyes" was all that some of the villagers would call him, as if they had never known his real name. Of course, these were the same ones who would spit between their fingers and make a sign to ward off evil when he passed. The other boys teased him mercilessly, of course, calling him "witchborn" and "moonchild."

As much as some of the villagers feared Nils, once he reached a certain age he found that others—specifically young women—were irresistibly drawn to him. This caused him no small distress. It was not that he didn't like having girls follow him around; part of him rather enjoyed it. But they would follow whether he wanted them to or not, and—even worse—whether or not they already had boyfriends.

For a peace-loving boy, he had an astonishing number of fights.

When Nils was sixteen he went to his mother and said, "It is time for me to make my way in the world. I must leave you now."

And though she wept, she knew that he was right.

She offered him gold to help him on his travels, but he would not take it, for it still filled him with horror, though he could not say why.

The day he left home Nils had not gone far into the forest when he realized that Sylvie, one of the girls from town, was following him.

"What are you doing?" he asked.

"I don't know," Sylvie replied, seeming not only confused by the question but startled to find herself alone with him in the wild. "It's just that—well, I thought you were leaving, Nils, and the idea scared me. Our town will not be the same without you—without your eyes." Reaching out a trembling hand, she stroked his cheek.

Before Nils could think of what to say he heard a furious roar. Looking past Sylvie's shoulder he saw her father, a beefy man with large fists and an even larger temper, racing toward them.

Feeling no need to prove his valor, Nils turned and fled, running as far and as fast as his feet would carry him. He dashed through the darkening woods, vaulting over fallen logs, splashing through crystal streams, stumbling over rocks and root-rippled ground, until at last he flung himself down beneath a vast old oak, where he lay clutching his side and gasping for breath.

He had been there for some time before the tree began to speak to him.

"You are different," it said, in a voice that seemed to come from the earth itself, rising in slow waves that Nils heard not with his ears but with his very skin.

"I know," said Nils ruefully.

"Don't . . . talk . . . so . . . fast," replied the tree, speaking so deliberately that it took four hours to finish the sentence. "Just . . . *listen.*"

So Nils, who felt as if he had grown roots himself, lay still and listened, slowly and deeply, in a way he never had before. And as he lay there, nestled in the tree's roots, it murmured to him the forest secrets, telling him it had waited hundreds of years for a human who could hear it.

"You have a long road ahead," said his new friend. "Seeds that are just sprouting will be trees many times your height before your heart will be at peace. You must learn to sing four things: the songs of the Earth, the Fire, the Water, and the Air. Three to save a life, the last to put your own soul at rest. This I know from the soil on my roots and the sun on my leaves, from the rain and the wind, which carry me news."

This took many days and nights to say, of course, and Nils stayed all this time without moving, locked in a sort of trance.

Finally the tree fell silent, and Nils stretched as if waking from a dream. He looked around.

The woods were dark, and he had no idea how long he had been here, nor, in truth, where he was.

"Well, my lad," he said to himself, "you've done it this time. But morning will come soon enough."

He was gathering some leaves to make a rough mattress when he noticed an ugly little face peering over one of the thick roots that rumpled the ground around him. He caught his breath and held motionless, afraid of frightening his visitor. He knew those eyes; they were the eyes he had seen from the time he was little. But now, at last, he could see the face that went with them, and he knew it was because the tree had changed him, taught him to see more slowly.

The eyes blinked and began to back away.

"Don't go," whispered Nils, his voice low but filled with urgency.

The creature ducked behind one of the thick roots. Nils strained his ears but could hear not the slightest rustle in the leaves. He counted ten long breaths, then said softly, "Are you still there?"

"*No!*"

Nils laughed. "Good. I was afraid you were going to stay and bother me all night long."

"You're not supposed to be able to see me," said the voice querulously. "No one can see us these days."

"Well, I didn't used to be able to see you," confessed Nils. "Just your eyes."

"As if that's not enough! Well, since you've already seen me, there's no point in hiding." And with that the creature climbed over the root. Not quite two feet high, it stood, hands on hips, staring at Nils defiantly.

"What are you?" Nils asked in astonishment.

"You can't tell?" replied the little man, sounding more irritated than ever. "Look at these ears!"

And, indeed, his ears were of interest, since they were pointed and at least twice as large as would have seemed normal for the size of his head.

"Look at these hands!"

The creature held out his hands, which were corded with veins. The fingers were long, the knuckles thick and knobbly.

"Look at this nose!" he fairly shrieked, plucking at the oversized sausage that grew between his eyes. "I'm a goblin, you fool. A goblin! And now that you've seen me, I'll have to take you to the land below."

"I should probably tell my mother before we go," said Nils.

The goblin sighed. "You really are a bit of a simpleton,

aren't you? No one gets to leave a message before taking such a journey!"

Suddenly Nils heard mutterings and stirrings all about him. A moment later he saw dozens of pairs of eyes—and a moment after that the goblins those eyes belonged to. With a cry, the ugly creatures rushed forward and snatched him off the ground. As Nils thrashed and struggled and cried out for help, they scampered across the forest floor, bearing him on their shoulders. Their little hands were incredibly strong, and fight as he might Nils could not escape.

What the goblins did not understand was that if they had only asked, Nils would have been perfectly happy to go with them on his own. He was eager to see new places, in the hope that he might, at last, find what he was searching for.

Moonlight lay in silver puddles upon the forest floor. The branches of the trees cast strange and threatening shadows. Nils's captors followed a stream to a waterfall that hid the mouth of a deep cave; when they scampered behind the falls, Nils had passed from the world we know to the strange and secret world of the goblins, which they call Nilbog.

Down they went, through secret stony passages, deep into the earth. Sometimes they traveled in darkness complete, sometimes on paths lit by torches topped with flickering flames of green, and more than once through caverns where the only light came from thick shelves of fungus that glowed pale blue.

The goblins came at last to the vast cavern where their king's castle had been built. They carried Nils across the drawbridge, through the gate, and into the presence of the king, who sat upon a throne carved from stone and clutched a ruby scepter while he scowled at the world.

"Why have you brought this human here?" demanded the king.

"He can see us!" cried the goblin to whom Nils had first spoken.

This so startled the king that he dropped his scepter. "Put him down," he ordered.

Immediately, the goblins let go of Nils, who fell to the floor with a painful thump.

The king stepped down from his throne to stare at him. "You have strange eyes," he said at last. "So perhaps it is true. Can you really see us?"

"I can," said Nils, trying to keep his voice from quaking.

"Prove it!"

So Nils described the king, telling him every detail of how he looked, from the wart at the end of his wobbly nose to the curving claws at the tips of his thick green toes.

To Nils's astonishment, the king began to weep. "At last!" he cried. "At last! It's been so long since anyone could see us that I had begun to fear we no longer existed. For you, my boy, a great boon is in order! Follow me!"

With goblins capering behind them, the king led Nils to the treasure chamber of Nilbog. Throwing wide the great doors he cried, "Take what you wish, lad. Anything you want is yours!"

Nils gasped. The room was filled with all things strange and wonderful, with goblin gold and massive gems, with swords and spears and kitchen knives, with shields and crowns, and enchanted jewels that whispered their names in the night. But as he looked, only one thing caught his heart, a plain harp made of dark wood that sat at the edge of the chamber. He remembered what the tree had told him, that he must learn to sing. So he plucked the harp from the pile, saying, "I'll take this."

"But it is worth hardly anything," said the king.

"It is what I want."

"It doesn't even have all its strings," protested the king, eager to have Nils take something finer and more precious. "See, the longest one is broken. Take something else."

"You have offered a boon," said Nils stubbornly, "and this is what I would like. May I have it?"

"I suppose so," grumbled the king. "But never say the goblins were stingy with you."

"You have given me what I wanted," replied Nils, clutching the harp to his chest. "That is generous enough."

"Let us at least teach you our songs," said the goblin king.

"Are they the songs of the Earth?" Nils asked hopefully. "I have been told that is what I must learn."

"What else would they be?" asked the king.

So Nils agreed to stay.

He spent three years with the goblins, listening to their songs and practicing on the harp. He had hoped the instrument would be magic and play with beauty the moment his fingers touched its strings. But this was not so, and Nils spent many hours learning to coax sweet music from it, trying not to be vexed by the missing string.

When he had learned all the songs of the Earth and could also play the harp passably well, the goblins placed a magic on the instrument to keep it safe from harm, then pointed him to a path and told him it would take him to the surface.

What they neglected to tell him was that there was a dragon along the way.

This was not malice on their part. The dragon, whose name was Gorefang, was the last dragon on Earth. He had been slumbering for so long he had been forgotten by everyone, even the other dragons, who had left for another world long ago. In fact, he himself had almost forgotten he existed. But when Nils came stumbling into his cave Gorefang roused himself. With flames flickering at the edges of his nostrils he grumbled, "What do you want . . . human?"

"I wish I could tell you. But I do not really know, which is why my heart knows no rest."

"And why do you have such strange eyes?"

Though Nils did not care to tell the story of what had happened when he was young, one does not lie to a dragon.

"A sad tale," murmured Gorefang at last. "No wonder you are restless." Shifting one massive claw so that it pointed at the harp Nils carried, he said, "It has been long since I heard music. Play for me."

"I know only the songs of the Earth. I'm not sure they would please a dragon."

"They'll do for a start. When you have sung those until I am tired of them, I will teach you the songs of

Fire. After all, we have plenty of time." With that, Gorefang shifted one vast, scaly wing so that it blocked the passage out.

With a sigh, Nils began to strum the harp. His music was better now than when he first picked it up, but still not what he wanted.

When he had played the songs he knew many times over, Gorefang yawned and said, "Enough. They were fine, but I cannot bear to hear them anymore. It's time you learned some new ones." And for the next three years Gorefang taught Nils the songs of Fire, which could set a heart aflame.

During those years, Nils drank from cold underground streams and ate little more than mushrooms and blind fish, though the dragon would toast them until they were quite tasty.

One day Gorefang closed his eyes and said, "I'm tired, and I've taught you all the songs I know. It is time for you to go."

Nils thanked the dragon seven times, then strapped the harp to his back and continued on his way.

His skin was pale now from his years underground, and he was more restless than ever, for something still gnawed at his heart, though it was nothing he could name.

222 · BRUCE COVILLE

When he had finally made his way to the surface he found himself at the edge of the northern sea. After gazing out at its vast gray surface, he sat upon a rock and began to sing, first the songs of the Earth, then the songs of Fire. They were lovely, even though he was hampered by the missing string.

While he was singing the fourth of the songs of Fire he heard a splash. Looking down, he saw a mermaid, her gold green hair floating like a fan over the water, her great fish tail clearly visible beneath the waves. She sang to him. He responded with one of the dragon's songs. She sang again, and beckoned, and with no thought for life or future Nils clambered down the rocks and into the water. The mermaid gazed into his silver eyes, then twined her arms around his neck and pulled him to the bottom of the sea, where she gave him a shell that let him breathe.

For three years Nils lived beneath the waves with the mermaid, and was her love, and they taught each other songs. But at the end of that time he grew restless, because his heart was still hungry. So the mermaid carried him to the surface and let him go, kissing him once for love and biting him once for anger before she sped him on his way.

So now Nils knew the songs of the Earth and the songs of Fire and the songs of the Water, and he wandered the north, going from village to village, singing for his supper. He had learned to play his harp quite beautifully by this time, and the missing string bothered no one but himself, because he was the only one who knew there were still songs he could not play, and chords beyond those his harp could sound. Still, his appearance troubled people, for they had never seen anyone so pale, much less one with eyes of silver.

As the decades passed, his hair became silver as well. Even in age he was beautiful, though in a strange and distant way, and everywhere he went at least one maiden would try to follow when he left. To stop her, he would sing a song so laced with loss and longing that she would sit by the side of the road and weep, unable to move. Then he would go forward alone.

Finally one maiden, bolder or more sly than others, followed him at a greater distance. He didn't realize she had done so until late at night, when he woke to find her on the opposite side of his dying campfire, staring at him with more curiosity than love, which he found refreshing.

"Why do you never stay in one place?" she asked.

The wind sang gently through the tops of the pine trees. The stars blazed in an ebony sky. And Nils's heart nearly burst with the question.

"I'm looking for something," he whispered.

"What?"

"I don't know."

"You would be a dangerous man to love."

"You could not pick anyone worse."

"My name is Ivy Morris, and I will walk for a while with you."

Despite his efforts to turn her away, the girl traveled with Nils for a year and a day. When he sang the song that had stopped the others in their tracks—which he did more than once—she continued walking, tears streaming down her face, murmuring, "I understand, for I am a wanderer, too."

Finally Nils wrote a new song, just for her. He called it "Song of the Wanderer," and it spoke of both their lives:

Across the gently rolling hills
Beyond high mountain peaks
Along the shores of distant seas
There's something my heart seeks

But there's no peace in wandering
The road's not made for rest
And footsore fools will never know
What home might suit them best

Ivy thanked him for the song.

The next day she was gone.

To the south, the world was changing as the age of machines crept on, transforming the earth in more ways than the people who were building and making and inventing could begin to understand. But in the northern forest Nils continued his wandering, spending less and less time in the villages and more time on the mountainsides, trailing the splashing streams, sitting on high promontories, singing only to the wind and the eagles.

And then one night, standing on a high hill and looking down at a crystal stream, Nils saw at last the thing he desired, the thing he had sought all these years, the thing he had longed for without knowing what it was he longed for, the thing his family had wronged so badly, so long ago.

He saw a unicorn.

Nils stood as if frozen while he watched it drink from the clear, cold water. Its coat glowed like white fire in the moonlight. Its creamy mane was like the froth on the waves of the northern sea where he had swum with his mermaid love, and its horn was a spiraled lance that seemed carved from the jewels of the earth. The sight of the creature filled him with such terrible longing that he could not speak.

When the unicorn turned from the stream he followed it, much as the girl named Ivy had followed him, though at a greater distance. He did not want it to know he was there. Not yet. Not yet.

It was not hard for Nils to trail the creature, for his heart was so tied to it that even when it was beyond the edge of his vision he could sense it. But Nils was not the only one stalking the unicorn. One afternoon as he came over a ridge and saw, as he knew he would, the unicorn in the green valley below, he saw something else, too. Something that filled him with cold terror.

It was a Hunter. Not just a man out hunting for his family. This was one of his own family, a man like his father who had but one mission in life—to find and slay the unicorns.

That was bad enough. Even worse, he had already captured this unicorn. It was an old story, one that Nils knew well. In the clearing stood a maiden. The unicorn had come to her, as a unicorn always will to a maiden in the woods, and she had slipped a golden bridle over his head, putting him in her power. Now she held him while the Hunter approached, spear in hand, ready to strike the final blow.

Nils was too far away to stay the Hunter's hand.

So he did the only thing he could, the only thing he knew.

He sang.

Taking his harp from his back, he sang the saddest song he knew, using every trick he had learned from goblin, from dragon, from mermaid, every bit of skill he had gathered in the decades since he first touched the harp.

The Hunter hesitated. His hands began to tremble.

Nils started forward, singing more softly now, intimately, caressing the Hunter's heart with the pain that had clutched his own for all these years, crafting his song like an arrow to pierce the other, and pouring into its notes all he knew of loss and longing.

The Hunter turned and stared at Nils in wonder. Then he dropped his spear, fell to his knees, and began to sob, releasing a flood of sorrow that had been locked in his heart from the first time his father had beaten him.

Nils walked past the sobbing Hunter, past the terrified girl.

"I have been seeking you for a long time," he said as he slipped the golden bridle from the unicorn's head.

The silver-eyed creature did not answer, but knelt in a clear invitation. Nils climbed on its back, and they fled through the forest, leaving Hunter and maiden far behind. When they were many miles away the unicorn stopped and Nils slid to the ground.

The unicorn turned to him, and Nils, who would have done anything for the beast, suffered anything for it, did not move at all when it stepped toward him, pointed its horn directly at his chest, and pierced the flesh above his heart.

Nils was sure he was about to die. To his astonishment, what happened instead was that the unicorn was able to speak to him.

To his sorrow, its voice was filled with horror.

"Something has happened to you," it said. "You've been touched by something, changed by something. You have—I don't know what this means—you have a bit of unicorn in you."

Nils's shame was so great, his first thought was to turn and run. But he could not leave the presence of the unicorn.

Nor could he stay silent.

So he told the story of what had happened when he was young, and his father had slain the unicorn. As he spoke he began to weep, something he had not done since he was four years old. He wept even more when the unicorn wept, too—and still harder when it placed its horn across his shoulder and murmured, "Whatever forgiveness you need, I grant."

In the storm of weeping that followed, Nils shed all the tears that had been locked inside since the moment he had swallowed the unicorn's flesh, tears for himself, for his mother, even for his father: tears of guilt, tears of rage, tears of loss.

He wept until there was no more silver in his eyes, and they were once again as they had been when he was a boy, as blue as the northern skies. And where each tear fell a flower grew, a little white flower that grows to this day in the northern hills, and which herb women call Heart's Ease.

When at last he was done with weeping, the unicorn, whose name was Cloudmane, and who was the first female unicorn ever to act as Guardian of Memory, said, "Pluck a hair from my tail."

Nils blinked. "Why would you want me to do that?"

She nudged him playfully and said, "Because your harp is in need of a string."

So Nils did as she said. The silver hair was gossamer thin, but stronger than steel, and when he had used it to string his harp, he ran his fingers over it and heard at last the sound he had been waiting so many years to hear. Then he wept once more, this time for joy.

Nils traveled with Cloudmane for three years. In that time she taught him the songs of the unicorns, which are the songs of the Air, and his heart was at peace.

When Cloudmane had taught him the last of the songs she knew, Nils bid her good-bye. Then he climbed to the top of a mountain, where he sat himself down and, looking out at the world, sang and sang, until at last he could sing no more.

A NOTE FROM THE AUTHOR

THIS BEING my third solo collection, I suppose I can no longer claim to find the short story an unnatural form. Even though my brain generally seems to think in novel-sized ideas, I actually like the discipline required for a short story, which forces me to do more with less. The odd result is that I end up doing what I think is some of my best writing this way.

For those who care about such things, here are a few notes on where this batch came from.

I originally wrote the opening story, "In Our Own Hands," as a booklet for adult literacy training. (My hometown, Syracuse, is one of the epicenters of adult literacy, having been headquarters for both Laubach Literacy and Literacy Volunteers of America, which eventually merged into ProLiteracy Worldwide.) Later I rewrote it for *Bruce Coville's Alien Visitors*. I've rewritten it yet again for this collection, and I think it has now found its final shape. I know the unresolved ending bothers some people, but to me that's the point of this kind of story. (And, of course, you have to tip your hat to Frank Stockton's "The Lady or the Tiger" whenever you try something like this.)

"What's the Worst That Could Happen?" came about because my friend James Howe was putting together an anthology called *13*—a collection of stories and poems about that joyful, excruciating first year of being a teenager, when so much is in uproar and turmoil. It may seem odd to have a story that is neither science fiction, nor fantasy, nor horror in this collection, but heck, what could be more horrifying than being thirteen? (Joke! *Joke!*) To write it I had to look back on my own thirteenth year, and while I didn't fall off a stage—that particular humiliation waited until I was in my forties—more of this is based on real life than I care to detail.

"In the Frog King's Court" was also written at the request of a friend, in this case the wonderful Nancy Springer, who was putting together a collection of frog stories to be shamelessly called *Ribbiting Tales*. My brain being what it is, a story about a werefrog was almost inevitable. The title plays off a story called "The Court of the Summer King" that Jennifer Roberson wrote for *The Unicorn Treasury,* one of my own anthologies. The difference is that Jennifer's story was lovely and profound, while this one is mostly goofy. But I really enjoyed doing it.

In the 1990s I edited a series of twelve anthologies for Scholastic that I refer to as Bruce Coville's Books of [Whatever]. (For "Whatever" you can fill in "Monsters," "Ghosts," "Spine Tinglers," and so on.) Before we go on, I'd like to say that while no one who knows me would deny I have a vast and sometimes appalling ego, I'm not so vainglorious to have come up with that title structure myself. It was the publisher's fault.

Anyway, two of these stories were written for those anthologies. Both were inspired, at least in part, by my daughter, Cara, who is the model for Nina ("Nine") Tanleven, the main character in "The Ghost Let Go." Nine's pal, Chris, was based on Cara's best friend, and her dad, Henry, is loosely based on, um, me. Nine and Chris appear in three novels. Chronologically, this story takes place between *The Ghost Wore Gray* and *The Ghost in the Big Brass Bed.*

The seed for "The Thing in Auntie Alma's Pond" came from a conversation Cara and I had when we were out walking one night. As we strolled past some dark water, she mentioned to me that she had always been terrified of the little pond where the kids used to swim when we visited her "Auntie Wilma." I got to thinking about that pond when it was time to write my story for *Spine Tinglers*. This is what came out.

I wrote "The Hardest, Kindest Gift" for my anthology *Half-Human*. The idea for the book, as is probably obvious, was to collect stories about half-humans: centaurs, mermaids, fauns, and so on. For my own story I turned to one of the more obscure of the half-humans, but one I found particularly haunting because of the longing and sense of tragedy that attaches to her. The text that appears here is considerably expanded from the first printed version.

The three remaining stories—"The Mask of Eamonn Tiyado," "Herbert Hutchison in the Underworld," and "The Boy with Silver Eyes"—make their print debut in these pages.

The first and third of these were written to perform with the Syracuse Symphony, something that is one of the great joys of my life. That "Eamonn Tiyado" was done for a concert we performed around Halloween should be no surprise. The music came from Liadov, Debussy, Holst, and Stravinsky. (The story's title is a hideous pun. In case it went right by you—as well it should have!—I'll give you a hint: The source is one of Edgar

Allan Poe's most well-known stories.) For "The Boy with Silver Eyes" the music came mostly from the great Norwegian composer Edvard Grieg. The story itself is connected to the world of the Unicorn Chronicles.

Finally we have "Herbert Hutchison in the Underworld," which is like the dark twin of "The Box," the story that opened the first of these collections, *Oddly Enough.* This one started to take shape in my head in what I call the "twilight time"—that time between sleep and full wakefulness.

A final note: All of the previously published stories have been revised, sometimes quite extensively, for these pages. For guidance in this process, I have to thank my editor, Allyn Johnston, and her erstwhile assistant, Beth Jacobsen, as well as my writing pal, Tamora Pierce.

When I was starting out, I loved to write but found revising painful. Now I find the initial writing hard but love the chance to revise.

Just another of life's ongoing oddities.

But I think that's my favorite thing about being alive.

It's just so odd!